TWO SHORT
STORIES

The Artwork
and
Seven Days with Miljana

Minna Tumbuleri

authorHOUSE®

AuthorHouse™
1663 Liberty Drive
Bloomington, IN 47403
www.authorhouse.com
Phone: 1-800-839-8640

First published by AuthorHouse 9/27/2011

ISBN: 978-1-4670-2699-4 (hc)
ISBN: 978-1-4670-2700-7 (sc)
ISBN: 978-1-4670-3822-5 (e)

Library of Congress Control Number: 2011916613

Printed in the United States of America

Edited by Hari Krishnan
Cover Design by plananddesignsite.com

To my dear parents

The Artwork

Chapter 1

Jane was driving back home after her office holiday party. It was past midnight, and as she neared home, she felt a weird knotting sensation in her stomach. It made her worry about the food she had eaten at the party. She wondered if it was the shrimp cocktail.

Soon as she got home, she popped some antacid tablets and prepared to turn in for what remained of the night. She dozed off almost immediately after she hit the bed, but was awakened by a severe abdominal cramp. Instinctively, she reached out for the cell phone on the nightstand and called her sister Jennifer. "Jane, it's three-thirty in the morning! I have an early meeting at work. Why are you calling me this late?" Jennifer was clearly alarmed.

"Jen, I'm in real pain, my stomach really hurts. I think it's the shrimp I ate at the party last night," Jane managed to say.

"Take the herbal supplement I gave you a few weeks ago," she said. "If you don't feel better, call me. I will come over to take you to the ER." Jen realized that her sister sounded very worried as she urged Jane to try drinking lots of water.

Feeling reassured just talking to her sister, Jane took the herbal supplement and returned to the bed, hoping the pain would subside. When her buzzer sounded and she slowly reached out to turn it off, Jane still felt the pain in her stomach, though not as severe. She decided to call her doctor's office immediately.

To her dismay, she learned that her physician was on vacation for the week. The nurse, to whom she explained the situation, suggested their office could refer her to a specialist, in this case a gastroenterologist. Jane called the specialist's office and managed to get a noon appointment on a very busy day at the clinic. Jennifer promised to take time off to drive her there.

Jane decided to lie down; as there was not much else she could bring herself to do with the nagging pain. She was regretting that she had eaten the shrimp appetizer at the party, when she heard the car honk outside. Her sister was already there to take her to the clinic. She wore her long brown coat, grabbed her keys and locked the house as she headed down to her ride.

Jennifer appeared flustered as usual but certainly looked concerned when she saw Jane. She helped Jane to the back seat and they drove off to the doctor's office. Jennifer looked in the rear view mirror and said, "Honey, I have another meeting at 1 pm. I will have to drop you off at the doctor's office. It's not much of a drive and I will be back to pick you up. Can you wait for me there? I brought along some soup for you."

Just like Jen to have taken the time to make soup while juggling her many tasks and meetings. "Sure, I'll wait," Jane answered softly.

"Did you have too much to drink?" Jen asked.

"No, I'm pretty sure it's the shrimp. I almost knew something was wrong with it and should have stayed away from it" Jane responded with frustration.

"Don't worry, you'll be fine," said Jen as she looked in the rear view mirror again while slowing down as they approached the medical center. She did look worried to Jane as she sped away after dropping Jane off at the entrance.

Jane approached the front desk and was greeted by the receptionist who asked for her name. "Jane Reynolds, I have a 12 pm appointment with Doctor Stoker," Jane responded, glancing at her watch.

The receptionist clacked furiously on the computer keyboard for a full minute and said, "Your PCP's office has sent us your information, so you are all set. Please take a seat and a nurse will be with you shortly."

There was only one vacant seat in the crowded lounge and Jane sat thankfully on it. She started browsing the old magazines, trying to ignore the pain. When it seemed like the wait could go on forever, a nurse appeared at the reception and called out Jane's name. Jane rose up and walked slowly to her. "Hi, my name is Beth, I'm your nurse. Sorry about the delay. We have quite a few patients today," the nurse muttered apologetically.

She led the way across the narrow corridor past several examination rooms. She led Jane to a bigger room and said, "You may please wait in this room. This is Dr. Stoker's office. I'm afraid all examination rooms are full. Please feel free to read the magazines. And yes, you can relax on his chair – I'm sure he won't mind," she grinned and closed the door behind her.

Chapter 2

Soon as the nurse left, Jane walked towards the cozy chair near the window. She slumped in the chair and took in the beautiful view of the snow-laden trees from the window. She turned around and adjusted slowly to the room and its contents. Jane noticed several volumes of medical practice books and a color diagram of the digestive tract on the wall. She studied the mundane diagram and the labels in detail, starting at the esophagus and traveling down to the colon. She already felt tired.

Jane let her gaze wander away lazily from the diagram. A framed painting, almost hidden behind the office desk, suddenly caught her attention. She walked towards the desk and without hesitation, pulled the heavy painting and leaned it against the wall.

The light from the window illuminated the painting and she simply stared at it, kneeling on the floor. "Wow!" she thought, "It almost looks like a painting but has inlaid ivory all over it. I am not even sure what to call it." It was a framed 4 feet by 3 feet painting with what looked like ivory seamlessly inlaid within. It was a portrait of a beautifully adorned woman under a large tree on a riverbank. She had never seen anything like this before.

She admired the simple beauty of the woman in the painting. The young woman wore a large golden nose ring. A thin gold chain hung from the nose ring across her face all the way to the hair above her left ear. She wore earrings and necklaces studded with precious stones. She was seated on a boulder under a large tree, with one leg on the boulder and the other hanging down, her body leaning to one side. Several studded bangles and bracelets adorned her left hand while her right hand was bereft of jewelry. Broken bangles lay scattered on the earth near her feet.

The artist had captured the hauntingly deep sorrow of the young woman who had a tear trickling down one cheek, her head bent slightly downwards. She had strikingly beautiful features. Her light caramel complexion was accentuated by the blue veil that was draped over her back and rested on part of her head. The veil was embroidered with small precious stones and was part of her exquisite blue skirt and blouse ensemble. Her slender waist was bare and her lustrous black hair flowed in tresses all the way to her waist.

The artist had used ivory generously. It was intricately embedded for the leaves, stones, the setting sun and the birds in the sky. The ivory tones captured the glimmer from the setting sun while the twilight hues from the brush strokes heightened the deepness and melancholy of the setting. There was a beautiful ancient structure on the bank of the river, in the background. With elaborately crafted spires and flags, it appeared to be an ancient temple.

"This must be an artwork from India. How fascinating and

rich it looks!" she wondered. Jane was surprised to see *Richard Brooks, 1783* inscribed on the bottom right corner and *Sati Gita* in the same handwriting, on the bottom left of the painting. "This is so old, it must be very valuable. What is it doing on the floor?" she wondered.

As Jane was admiring the artwork, she felt drawn to the painting in an inexplicable way. "There's something about this painting. I just can't take my eyes off it." She was interrupted by a short knock on the door followed by a woman's voice asking, "Can I come in?" Jane hastily pushed back the painting behind the desk, as she had found it before. She went back to the chair, just before the nurse opened the door.

Chapter 3

The nurse said, "Hi Jane! Sorry about the delay. Dr. Stoker is running late, he has one more patient ahead of you. I'm going to quickly check your vital signs." While examining her for blood pressure, the nurse asked, "Will you be going out for lunch or will you wait here? Just so you know; there is a cafeteria on this level."

"I will wait here," said Jane, "I have some soup with me." The nurse smiled and left, silently closing the door behind her.

Jane took the opportunity and pulled out the artwork from behind the desk. Once again, she found herself staring at it and thinking, "Why do I like this painting so much? Why am I drawn to it so strongly?" She gazed at it longer, taking in the details unhurriedly.

She was surprised to see so many things she had not noticed the last time, including a peacock near the tree with its vividly colored plumage. "What an incredibly serene setting, with this magnificent large tree on the riverbank?" The tree trunk alone was several feet wide and there were numerous gnarled branches drooping vertically to the ground and taking root in the earth. She realized they had no leaves, unlike the other branches on the tree. Her gaze was drawn back to the sadness in the young woman's eyes. "Why is she so sad and lost?" thought Jane, as she experienced a sudden feeling of sorrow. She felt a strange connection to the woman's pain and suffering.

Suddenly the door opened without warning. "Hi, I'm Dr. Stoker," said the tall, middle-aged man who entered the room. Jane stood still and forced a smile. She was caught unawares and was unsure how to push the painting back to where it was. "You are Jane, right?" said the doctor, glancing at the folder in his hand. Jane stepped forward to shake his hand and introduced herself, "Hello Doctor, I'm Jane Reynolds."

"Please take a seat. Sorry for making you wait so long, but I see you've kept yourself busy. Tell me about your pain. How are you feeling now?" Dr Stoker asked.

"I've been having stomach cramps since last night. I think it's something I ate," said Jane as she sat on the examination table. Dr Stoker examined her, all the while asking her questions about the food she had eaten the previous night and her food habits otherwise.

He sat down and explained to her that she seemed to have a very mild form of food poisoning and that she did not need any medication. After giving her diet advice and tips to handle the pain, he asked, "Any questions?"

"As a matter of fact, yes doctor," said Jane haltingly and not knowing quite how to ask him. She went ahead anyway. "I have quite a few questions, but I'm afraid they are about the painting. I'm sorry I pulled it out from behind your desk without asking you. It's such a beautiful art. I have not seen one like this…" continued Jane.

"The artwork from India?" interrupted Dr. Stoker. "An old friend gave it to me. He went to Harvard Medical School with me, a very interesting man. As far as I can tell, he was one of the best cardiologists in Massachusetts," he paused. "Poor fellow died of a heart attack a few years ago," he said with a heavy sigh. "He came from one of the royal families in India," he continued. "Yes, that was Ritesh Kumar. He gave me this painting a few months before he returned to India. He wanted to set up a completely free state-of-the-art medical clinic for the poor in India."

"Why do you keep it on the floor and behind your desk?" Jane asked hesitantly, wanting to know more about the painting than about the man who gave the painting to Dr. Stoker. "Oh," he answered sheepishly, "I tried to hang it up a few times. The painting fell down and ripped our living room wall. My wife and I argued a lot over this painting. She never liked it, can you believe that?"

"I tried to hang it in my office but, as you can see there's not enough space here. It was sitting on the corner table, but then just about everybody in the medical center who came into my office was asking about it. So I had to hide it. I just don't have the time to discuss about the painting with office staff, nurses and patients," he stopped abruptly, realizing that he had given more than the necessary hint about the painting being a major distraction at his office.

Jane understood that there was no more room for querying him on the painting and that she had to leave. While she was gathering her stuff and getting ready to leave, Dr Stoker turned back and asked her, "I knew a James Reynolds from Belmont. Are you his daughter, by any chance?"

"Yes. How do you know him?" Jane asked. Stoker nodded his head and recollected, "I used to live two streets away from your house. I very clearly remember how you guys survived the fire. I saw your father on TV. If I recollect well, he did mention that you saved the family...right?"

"Yes, I am afraid I was the one, and I was just a ten-year old then. That makes it like, about seventeen years ago," Jane replied, a little surprised. "Sorry, I don't remember meeting you, but I'm glad to know we were neighbors at one time!"

Stoker rose from his desk and asked softly, "Jane, would you like to visit us for dinner sometime? My wife would love to meet you." Jane just couldn't refuse this sudden offer. "Thanks," she said excitedly, "I would love to come."

"That's great! If you are free this weekend, give me a call on Friday. I will let Christine know that you will be joining us for dinner. You can get my home and cell number from Wendy at the front Desk. I'll let her know."

Bidding farewell to Dr. Stoker, Jane walked out of the medical center, her mind filled with thoughts about the painting and the fire incident from the past. Still in a daze, she pulled out her beeping cell phone. She checked the text message and realized her sister had been waiting at the parking lot for over ten minutes. Jane hurriedly pulled on her coat, gloves and woolen cap as she rushed to the parking lot. She found Jennifer sitting in her car, parked not far from the entrance. Apologizing for making her wait, she sat in the passenger seat and stretched out her gloved hands to the dashboard to try and warm up from the biting cold outside. Jennifer raised her eyebrows and asked, "How did it go? You look well already."

Jane smiled and answered, "It's some form of food poisoning. The doctor wants me to take lots of water and rest. Thanks Jen, for taking time off just for me."

As Jennifer drove slowly and carefully through the snow filled streets of Needham on their way to Boston, she talked about her work, her colleagues and research projects. Jane was not listening to her sister. She was lost in thoughts about the painting. "Jane," said Jennifer, trying to get her attention, "Are you OK? You seem lost in thought."

Jane looked at her sister and immediately felt guilty for not paying attention to her. "Sorry, I'm just tired. It must be all the sleep that I missed last night. I really want to rest. I'm going to be just fine."

Jennifer sounded very concerned as she said, "You don't have to live in Boston, you know. Jack is no longer with you, so you have to move on. You were much stronger than me. You saved us from certain death when you were just a kid." Jane remained silent. Jennifer continued, "I want you to be strong, Jane. Forget your ex and take a break. Why don't you go to Florida and spend some time with Mom and Dad."

Not wanting to discuss this topic any further, Jane reassured her sister that everything was just fine and that she could handle life without her ex-boyfriend Jack. She told her that as a matter of fact, she no longer missed him that much. When they reached Jane's apartment building, she kissed her sister goodbye and stepped out of the car. As she walked up to her apartment, her mind was completely occupied with images from the painting at Doctor Stoker's office.

Chapter 4

The concierge greeted her as Jane walked into her apartment building. Jane walked straight to the elevators, totally oblivious to everything around her and leaving behind a very embarrassed concierge. She got off the elevator on the ninth floor. Her apartment had large windows with a stunning view of the Boston skyline. She stared out the window at the brightly lit skyline, preoccupied with an endless list of questions, "Why am I plagued by that painting?" "Why do I feel so helpless and empty? Who is that woman in the painting?" As the questions kept coming, Jane started to despair, "I need to get this out of my head...I feel like I'm going crazy." Jane tried to reason with her emotions, "I know I have been through a lot in the past few months. Maybe I just need to unwind."

Deciding to rest and relax for the rest of the day, Jane showered for a long time. She cooked Israeli couscous with some fresh vegetables and herbs. Remembering the doctor's advice, she filled a large glass of water and sat on the couch with a bowl of her warm dinner. She turned on the TV and started surfing channels till a news channel showing a raging fire caught her attention. The reporter was covering the news about a three-storied house on fire in Boston and the successful rescue operations by the firemen.

As she watched the burning house on TV, vivid images of the woman in the painting flashed before her. *Sati Gita*, the woman in the painting was engulfed in flames and begging Jane with outstretched hands to save her. Jane watched in shock and horror as the fires raged around the burning woman who looked directly into Jane's eyes. Jane jumped off the couch, shuddering at this unnerving experience. She turned off the television, with her hands trembling.

Jane walked into her bedroom and turned on her laptop. She googled *Sati Gita* and scanned every result on the page but couldn't find a relevant match. She tried various phrases and combinations including *Sati Gita painting, Painter James Brooks* and clicked several links that took her nowhere. Exhausted, she dozed off on the desk.

In her sleep, Jane drifted into a dream. *She was walking on the banks of a river, dressed in a long white gown. She sees several young women dressed in colorful Indian clothes. They were talking and laughing as they carried brass plates filled with fruits and flowers. The girls walked to a large tree and made offerings to a statue under the tree. One of them, the woman in the painting, started laughing uncontrollably and fainted. The others rushed to her and surrounded her. All of a sudden, the air was filled with their sorrowful cries.*

Shocked and disturbed by what she witnessed, Jane runs towards the river only to see her old house in Belmont burning. The scene is now the fire in the kitchen of her childhood home in Belmont. She is a ten-year old, asleep in her bedroom. Her sister and parents are asleep as the fire slowly rages in the kitchen. She opens her eyes suddenly to see someone shaking her furiously to wake her up. It is the same young woman who fainted near the tree at the riverbank.

The buzzer blared and Jane woke up with a start. She squinted at the timer. It was six in the morning and Jane wondered how she had slept through the night on the chair. She slowly eased herself onto the bed and lay there, staring at the ceiling. "She saved us, she saved my family! She was the one who woke me up so I could save my family. What if she hadn't awakened me…?" Jane kept thinking, "Yes, that was her! The woman who woke me up on that fateful night was none other than the one in the painting."

Jumping out of her bed, Jane grabbed her cell phone and called her manager. She left him a voice message, "Bob, its Jane here. I'm not feeling well and would like to take sick time off for today and tomorrow. Please call me on the cell if you need to reach me."

Jane sat down once again on the desk, and renewed her search on the laptop to find more details about the painting. After several attempts leading to irrelevant links on different search engines, she returned to Google and, on a hunch, typed *"Richard Brooks, controversial painting, 1783."* The very first link in the listed search results read *"Controversial 1783 Painting by Richard Brooks."*

Chapter 5

Jane clicked on the link immediately, hoping to finally get some information. The page contained old maps of England and India. The text below read: Richard Brooks (1763 – 1783) was born in Norwich in the Norfolk County of England to Elizabeth and James Brooks. Richard had two sisters, Anna and Kate. The following is a story of the controversial painting by Richard Brooks.

In the summer of 1780, Richard's father, James Brooks, was deputed for a three-year assignment as an English teacher for a Muslim royal family in northern India. Richard was seventeen when they sailed to India. With the help and influence of the then Duke of Norfolk, James managed to arrange for his son, a commission as a painter at the royal court.

Richard was very excited to travel and live in a palace guesthouse. He had heard stories about the kings and nobles of India and his childhood dreams came true upon his arrival in India. Their family was accommodated in a guesthouse that was an annex to the palace with servants and facilities they had never enjoyed before. He felt like a prince.

Richard would go on long walks every morning with his assigned guard, Sakku Ram, who usually carried around the easel and painting supplies. Sometimes, he would spend several days travelling to places where he could capture nature and people in his paintings. On one of his travels with Sakku, he reached a temple near the Soane River in Bahar province. Enchanted by the natural beauty of the place, Richard settled down under a large banyan tree to paint, while Sakku Ram rested on the steps of the temple.

Enjoying the pleasant breeze and the humming of birds at the riverbank, Richards looked around the magnificent banyan tree and its gnarled branches. He noticed a little mound of earth close to the small boulder he was sitting on. He called out to Sakku Ram for help and started loosening the earth around the mound with a broken branch. To his sheer amazement, they unearthed a large wooden artwork with inlaid ivory. The artwork appeared to have been deliberately smashed even before it was buried beneath the mound. Richard and Sakku dug deeper and wider. They came across a cloth with writings in Sanskrit. Richard was completely intrigued by this new finding, and decided to return home with the artwork.

He locked himself in his room, painstakingly attempting to restore the damaged artwork. Unable to restore it after several days of work, he decided to copy the artwork to bring new life to it in the form of a painting. In his painting, he recreated the beautiful young woman from the artwork, sitting under the banyan tree on the very same rock he had been sitting on before spotting the mound. He added peacocks and birds in an evening sky with the setting sun in the background.

The woman in the artwork was sad and had a tear running down from one eye. Her hands were bare and broken bangles lay scattered on the ground. In his painting however, Richard adorned one hand with bangles. After finishing his painting, he spent days and nights looking at the beautiful woman in the painting and worrying about her. He talked to her, locked up in the room for days on end, wondering what made her sad.

Concerned about their son, James and Elizabeth had the royal physician examine Richard. He had not eaten in days and had fallen ill. Though he was extremely weak, his mind was filled with questions. He took the physician to his room and showed the painting and the damaged artwork. He showed him the cloth with the inscriptions that they found along with the artwork and quizzed him with a barrage of questions, anxious to know if the physician had any information about the artwork and why it was buried.

The physician asked Richard to rest on the bed. He sat on a chair beside him and carefully scrutinized the artwork and the inscription on the cloth. He then drew closer to Richard and began narrating the story of the damaged artwork.

The lady in the artwork was Gita, born to a very rich merchant in Bahar. She was one of the most beautiful women in her town. In the year 1543, the Mughal Emperor had assigned a nawab to rule parts of Bahar. The nawab had twelve sons. Ismail, the youngest and most handsome boy had set his eyes on Gita. They fell in love and met secretly every night at the banyan tree on the banks of the Soane.

As their romance blossomed, Gita's father, a very staunch Hindu, came to know about his daughter's exploits. He swiftly arranged her marriage to a merchant who was 30 years older than his daughter. On the wedding night, Gita wanted to elope with Ismail, but she was drugged and went through the marriage rituals in a semiconscious state. When she awoke the next morning, she was devastated. Unable to accept the blow dealt to her life, she tried to end it but her mother intervened. She emotionally blackmailed Gita that ending her life in this manner would guarantee the death of all her siblings. Gita was forced to accept married life and moved to her new husband's house.

Heartbroken, Ismail made several attempts to save the love of his life from the miserable marriage. The nawab learned of his son's situation and sent him abroad on a religious mission. When Ismail returned after three years, he still could not forget Gita. He secretly sent her a note asking her to meet him. Gita agreed to meet her true love. Fatefully, on the very same day that Gita was to secretly meet Ismail at night, her husband died of old age and ailments. His last words to his wife were, "You are free now."

At nightfall, Gita sneaked out of her home and with the help of her trusted maids, made her way to the banyan tree near the river Soane. She waited for her lover under the banyan tree, while her three maids spread out and stood guard. With tears in her eyes, Gita sat on a small rock under the banyan tree, fully dressed as a bride and adorned in bridal jewelry. After a short while, Ismail came to the riverbank. He stopped upon seeing her, moved to tears by the sight of his beloved after these years of separation and mesmerized by her beauty.

Ismail approached her, and kneeling before her, begged her to come away with him to share his love for her. Gita looked at him and cried. She told him that, as required by custom, she would have to perform "Sati" and join her husband in the *funeral pyre. He was to be cremated in the morning. If she defied, her family would not be spared.*

Gita was pouring out her sorrows to her lover and crying in his arms, when the maids started screaming. The nawab's guards came charging and took Ismail away. Gita fainted and fell to the ground. As per the horrific practice of the Sati custom, she was burnt alive the next day with her dead husband.

Unable to forget Gita, Ismail devoted all his time and energy to creating a beautiful wooden artwork depicting his last moments with Gita. He would never forget the sadness and helplessness on her face as she sat under the tree, decked in bridal attire and jewelry. Ismail took to drink and lived as a recluse, abandoning his royal life and home. He carried his artwork with him wherever he went.

One day he was attacked by some Hindu fanatics and killed. Ismail's artwork was half destroyed and buried, with a note, narrating the story of Gita and Ismail, near the same temple where he last met Gita.

Richard was shocked that there was still such a practice where a widow was burnt alive with her dead husband. He succumbed to his illness and died a few days later. After the loss of their only son, the bereaved parents decided to return to England with their daughters. They gave the painting to the Royal family and sailed back home.

The painting was a very controversial topic in India; it sparked many arguments and fights between the Hindus and Muslims and even the ruling British, when they intervened. After several thefts and attempts to destroy the painting, it was given to a

Royal family in Mysore. As years went by, the painting was forgotten. The Royal family of Mysore, that owned Richard's painting, had reported to the police that it was missing in the year 1945.

Chapter 6

Jane paused after reading the story on the website. She scrolled to the bottom and noticed the footnote - Content contributed by the Brooks Family, Norwich, England. She slowly raised her head away from the computer and looked to the left, at the window. She walked to the window and looked down at the people walking in the busy street below. Her mind was so engrossed in the story of the artwork that she failed to hear her cell phone ring.

Jane walked to her bathroom and looked at herself in the mirror. "I have to save her, the way she saved me. I'm going to call Dr. Stoker and meet with him today," she said to herself with urgency.

After her shower, Jane checked her cell-phone and realized that she had missed calls from her sister and from work. She found Dr. Stoker's cell number in her phone address book and called him. She had entered the number in her cell phone after getting it from the receptionist on her way out of Dr. Stoker's office the previous afternoon. Dr. Stoker answered the call immediately.

"Hi Dr. Stoker, this is Jane. How are you?" asked Jane.

"Hi Jane, how are you feeling? Hope you are much better, we are excited to have you come home this weekend," said Dr. Stoker.

"I'm feeling much better, thanks for asking. I'm sorry to disappoint you, but I think this weekend will be very difficult for me. I have not gone to work for a while, and have work piled up for the weekend. Can we meet tonight? I want to talk to you about the painting. I'm hoping we can meet tonight…" she paused.

"Sure, but Christine is out of town, visiting her sister. She won't be back until Friday. If it's all right with you, we can meet at Jimmy's at six-thirty. It's the building right next to my office," Jeff offered. Excited, Jane confirmed their meeting time and hung up.

Jane dressed quickly, picked up her cell phone and keys and headed to the elevator, closing the door behind her. At the parking garage, she got into her Volkswagen Beetle and drove out onto the crowded streets of Boston. *The Nights in White Satin* by Moody Blues was playing on her favorite radio station, and she drifted into memories of her boyfriend, her childhood, the fire incident and once again, the sorrowful expression of the woman in the painting. She looked in the rearview mirror and was startled to see the beautiful brown eyes of the young woman, crying out for help. She steadied herself in time to merge onto the westbound highway.

She looked at the banks of snow piled up on either side of the road and was thankful for the clear weather. She raised the volume as Santana's *Black Magic Woman* played. She wanted to be at Jimmy's on time and started thinking about the questions she would ask Dr. Stoker.

Arriving at Jimmy's, Jane parked her car in the lot behind the restaurant and walked around to the front entrance, excited and confused at the same time about her meeting. Doctor Stoker had made a reservation and a waitress led her to a table. While she glanced at the menu, sipping iced tea, her phone beeped showing missed messages. "Oh shoot!" she thought, "It's my sister!" She quickly read the missed text messages.

There were two from her sister and one from her parents asking her to call them back ASAP and that they were worried about her. Jane barely began texting a reply when she was interrupted by a man's voice "Jane?" She looked up to see Dr. Stoker standing right beside her dressed in a blue striped shirt and unbuttoned trench coat. Jane stood up and greeted him with a warm handshake. Dr. Stoker gave her a hug, took off his coat and settled down in the seat opposite to her.

"You look good, and healthy! I'm sure you are feeling great already, now that you have seen the painting," he said jokingly.

"Thanks, Doctor" Jane responded with a smile.

"Call me Jeff, I'm not here to examine you" he joked again.

"OK, Jeff. I can get used to that," said Jane.

Jeff asked softly, "So Jane, how are your parents? I met your father about a year before the fire incident. I remember the night we saw you on TV; you were this brave young girl who saved the family."

"Thanks for asking, my parents are doing very well. They are in Naples, Florida. I met them for thanksgiving. They are going on a Caribbean Cruise next week." Jane continued, "I'd better call them. My sister has sent me enough reminders already! Jen, my older sister, lives right here in Needham."

"You were the brave one!" exclaimed Jeff, holding Jane's hand affectionately. "My wife would have loved to talk to you; she was always talking about you to our son…"

"Jeff" interrupted Jane, "A lady woke me up on that fateful night. She was none other than the lady in the painting! If she hadn't awakened me, we would have died," she said firmly, looking at the doctor who was puzzled. "Jeff, I know I sound like a fool. And you, as a doctor are probably going to ask me to see a shrink. I'm here today to ask you for a favor, I want to buy the painting. Please don't say no," pleaded Jane.

Shocked by this unexpected request, Jeff pulled his hand away from Jane's, and was dumbfounded for more than a minute. They were interrupted by the waitress, who took their orders and left. Jane looked at Jeff earnestly, anticipating an answer.

"Jane, like I mentioned earlier, the painting was given to me by Ritesh, a very good friend of mine. It was given to me for safekeeping," Jeff began cautiously. He paused with his brows knitted in thought. He then continued, "Ever since I brought the painting home, my wife and I have had several arguments. She wanted me to get rid of it because my son would spend hours staring at it neglecting his homework. I gave my friend my word, to safeguard it as long as I can. There must've been a reason why he wanted me to keep it. I have had to literally hide it to avoid any theft or robbery."

Jeff paused in hesitation. He said, "I must tell you something. This painting was stolen a while ago from my home – there was a break-in and just the painting was taken. My son went into depression after that event, and believe it or not, one day it just appeared on the door step."

"Ritesh's wife lives in Belgium with her brother's family. If you want to know more about this painting and want to take it, she is the right person to talk to," Jeff continued.

"Belgium?" interrupted Jan, puzzled.

"Yes, I think she lives in Antwerp. Her brother is a diamond dealer there. Why don't you give me your e-mail, and I will send you her phone number and address. I haven't talked to her in a while. Maybe I can take the opportunity and tell her about you, so she's prepared." He stopped abruptly as the waitress returned and set their food on the table.

Jane gave her e-mail address to Jeff and expressed her interest to meet with Ritesh's wife in person. The rest of their conversation was cordial as they enjoyed the food. They left the crowded restaurant, and standing at the parking lot, Jeff said, "I will send you the address and contact information Jane, but I think you will have to let go. You should focus on your future and not the past; I'm sorry about the accident that happened to you and your family, but the point is - you guys are safe. You are safe."

Jane nodded, acknowledging Jeff's words. She was shivering in the chilly evening as she tried to put on her gloves, "Thanks Jeff, I just want the painting so badly. It's not about digging into the past; it's another woman's life. I know it sounds crazy, but I am just not able to explain why I want it," she said firmly.

Jeff nodded, trying unsuccessfully to convey that he understood. "I will be out of town for a week starting this weekend. I'm going to San Francisco for a conference. So, I will send you the address tonight. Good luck!" Jeff smiled and walked away.

Jane slowly walked to her car and got in as it started to snow. She leaned her head on the headrest with her eyes closed and sighed with relief. "I wish I can get the artwork! It is right here in the next building and yet seems so far away," she thought. She quickly started her car and drove out of the parking lot.

Jane called her parents and convinced them that she was doing well and keeping herself busy at work. She then called her sister. The line was busy, so she left a message, "Hey Sis! I'm driving to your place now. I will see you in about fifteen minutes."

It started snowing heavily as Jane navigated the snow-filled streets, her mind filled with childhood memories. She reminisced about her sister and herself throwing snowballs at each other and making snowmen together. Somehow, her thoughts trailed into a scene of some teenage girls playing around a banyan tree and running to the river, splashing water on each other. A girl decked in regal clothes and jewels, like a princess, was being chased by her playmates. She gleefully runs towards a large tree, stops in front of it and falls down crying.

Bee...eep. Jane's thoughts were abruptly interrupted by loud and continuous honking. She hit the brakes instinctively as a driver in a pickup truck yelled at her and drove by. To her horror, Jane realized she was on the wrong side of the street and veering close to the curb. She quickly swerved back onto her lane and tried to regain her composure. She took the next right turn onto the street where her sister lived.

Jane was warmly welcomed by her sister and niece. After playing with her niece for a while, Jane walked to her sister in the kitchen. "Jen, I need to talk to you. Can we go to your bedroom?"

"Sure, I'll be there in a minute," said Jen.

Jane waited in her sister's bedroom, looking at the pictures of her little niece on the wall. She asked Jane to close the door as she entered the bedroom. Jane recanted everything that had happened since her visit to the Doctor. She talked about the painting and her conversations with Dr. Stoker. "So you are sure this is the same lady you have talked about for several years?" asked Jen.

"Yes. I am positive!" Jane said firmly. She wanted to dispel any doubt in her sister's mind.

After a long pause Jen asked, "What will you do with the painting? What makes you feel you will save her, and from what? I find this a little confusing. If I know you, I am sensing where this is headed. Are you going to Belgium?"

"Jen, I know you are concerned. To answer your question, I don't know how I'm going to save her but I know she needs my help. I absolutely need that painting! I need to go to Belgium; I might leave tomorrow after I get the address from Dr. Stoker," said Jane with a fire in her voice. "I know you are worried, but please don't be. I will be just fine. I am going home now to book the tickets. I'll keep you posted, OK?" Jane reassured her sister.

Bidding them goodbye, Jane drove back to her home in Boston. She checked her e-mail and found Dr. Stoker's e-mail with the address and contact number in Antwerp. He also mentioned that he had called Ritesh's wife, Sharmila Kumar, informing her about Jane's impending visit to Belgium.

Jane immediately called the number given to her by Jeff. "Hello" said a voice in an Indian accent. "Hi! My name is Jane and I would like to talk to Mrs. Sharmila Kumar," she said. "This is Sharmila. Jane, I just got a call from Dr. Stoker, you can come to Antwerp anytime this week and call me when you get here, OK? I would like to meet you in person," Sharmila sounded as though she knew Jane for a long time. Jane realized that Sharmila did not want to talk any details on the phone. She asked Sharmila for the address and the best place to stay in Antwerp. Jane thanked her and hung up.

Jane called her travel agent and booked her flight through Swiss Air to Brussels, connecting in Zurich. She did a map search for the address where Ritesh's wife lived, and searched for a hotel nearby. She found the Lindner Hotel in Antwerp, Belgium that Sharmila had suggested. Jane asked her travel agent to reserve a room for two days there. Jane hastily packed her suitcase and settled down in her bed, hoping to get some sleep before her journey the next morning.

Chapter 7

Jennifer was there at the airport to see her off. Jane had called her sister and updated her about her travel plans the previous night. After bidding goodbye to her sister, Jane boarded the Swiss Airlines flight to Brussels. Soon after takeoff, she started browsing through the information about Antwerp and Brussels in the guidebook she purchased at the terminal newsstand. She could barely contain her excitement.

After a long flight and stopover in Zurich, Jane arrived at Brussels International Airport. After picking up her baggage, she headed to the information booth. The clerk at the information kiosk spoke fluent English and Jane was able to gather directions and travel information quite easily. With a street map in hand, she headed out of the airport to get a taxi.

It was a Mercedes taxicab, and the driver said "Hallo!" with a Dutch accent after opening the door. Jane tried to recollect how to say thank you in Dutch and hesitantly uttered, "*Dank u*". She then asked the driver, "*Spreek je Engels?*"

"Yes, but not like American, OK?" the driver smiled, looking at the rearview mirror. "Madam, where are we going?" he asked.

"Antwerpen, Lindner Hotel," Jane responded.

They exited the airport, briefly traveling on highway E40 and then headed onto highway E19. Jane looked out of the window, taking in the views and trying to read the town names as the signs whizzed past her - Elewijt, Weerede. Soon they arrived at the Lindner Hotel. Taking her baggage after paying the driver, Jane walked to the lobby to check-in.

The receptionist welcomed her, speaking fluent English with a French accent, and checked her into a junior suite. Jane entered her room on the seventh floor with beautiful views of Antwerp's *Grote Markt* and the Cathedral of Our Lady. She was totally enthralled by the beautiful diamond city and the million things that were happening all around. It seemed unusually warm out there. She reminded herself, "I'm on a mission, and I need to stay focused."

Jane slept for a couple of hours. She had been awake the entire length of the flight and the nap really helped her. She showered and dressed in comfortable jeans and shirt and a long sweater, letting her red hair down.

She headed down to the lobby and asked the receptionist "How do I get to this address? Would you be able to give me a map?" The receptionist gave Jane a map and highlighted the way to her destination on the map. It seemed pretty straightforward to Jane. Glancing at the clock above the front desk, Jane realized it was five in the evening. She quickly changed the time on her watch to the local time and stepped out of the lobby onto the bustling street.

Following the map, Jane walked on *Lange Leriusstraat* towards Stads Park, after a few blocks she arrived at the address she was looking for. It was a luxury apartment building facing the park.

She entered the building and greeted the uniformed concierge. She told him that Sharmila Kumar who lived in apartment 11906 was expecting her. The concierge dialed the number and spoke rapidly in Dutch. He hung up and looked up at Jane.

In a very strong Dutch accent he said, "She is on the way. She is coming down now. Please sit down." Thanking him, Jane sat on the couch; hoping her long journey would be worth it. She turned and looked out of the window to see the beautiful view of Stads Park.

The elevator arrived and Jane saw an elegant Indian lady, in her sixties, step out onto the lobby. She wore a pastel printed pink silk sari, and an elaborately embroidered woolen shawl. She was around five feet and seven, with a light brown complexion. She approached Jane and asked with a smile, "Jane Reynolds?"

"Yes, Hi!" responded Jane acknowledging with a handshake.

"I'm Sharmila, very nice to meet you. Dr. Stoker called me last night - quite late, actually. He told me that you will be visiting," she said and added, "Nobody comes to visit me."

"I'm glad you could meet with me, I really wanted to meet with you as soon as I could. I am sorry if I caused any inconvenience," said Jane, smiling apologetically.

"Not at all" said Sharmila in an Indian accent. "Do you mind if we step out? I'm not comfortable talking in my brother's house. I will take you to *Grote Markt*; it's a very beautiful place and just a short drive from here. Let's have dinner there!" Sharmila said excitedly.

Asking Jane to wait at the lobby while she got her car, Sharmila went back towards the elevators to get to the underground parking garage.

Within a few minutes, Jane was surprised to see her pull up at the front entrance in a gleaming black Mercedes. She was signaling Jane to get in. Jane got into the plush leather seat of the S500, and they drove towards central Antwerpen.

Driving swiftly through the narrow residential streets, Sharmila noticed Jane looking out at the streets, the people and the beautiful Dutch buildings. She asked, "Have you been here before?"

"No, I haven't. It's such a beautiful place."

"Yes indeed," Sharmila sounded quite excited, "It's the diamond center of the world. There are businessmen and tourists here the year round. That is the Central Train Station to your right," she pointed out to Jane.

Chapter 8

They drove towards Antwerp's *Grote Markt* and found a spot to park the car. Sharmila told Jane that they would need to walk a few blocks to a very good café. As they walked towards the center of *Grote Markt*, Sharmila showed Jane the Town Hall, the Cathedral of our Lady, and the famous Brabo fountain in the center of the paved plaza. They walked to a café located right in front of the Cathedral, and chose the farthest table that still had a splendid view. Just as they sat down at the table, Sharmila asked, "If you don't mind, can I ask you your age, Jane?"

"Not at all, I'm twenty seven." Jane was beginning to feel quite comfortable with Sharmila.

"If I was blessed with children, I would've had a daughter about your age," Sharmila said solemnly looking down at her hands and brushing aside her long gray hair from her shoulder. She cheered up almost immediately and continued, "So, why do you want the painting? Jeff did not give me any reason, and I didn't ask."

Jane told Sharmila about how she saw the painting hidden

behind Jeff's office desk and how after that day, she was haunted by the woman in the painting. She told Sharmila about her dreams and disturbing visions and the uncanny resemblance of the woman in the painting to the young girl who woke Jane up when she was a ten-year old and saved Jane and her family from a fire disaster. She described the fire incident to Sharmila. Somehow, Jane didn't feel the least bit uncomfortable sharing her innermost feelings about the woman in the painting with Sharmila. In fact, she was quite relieved to express what she had been going through since the time she laid her eyes on the artwork.

After intently listening to Jane, Sharmila looked into Jane's eyes and said flatly, "Jeff will never part with the artwork. He will not sell it to you at any cost. Can you believe he lost his son on account of that artwork, and still did not let go of it?" Sharmila stopped abruptly when she saw the shock in Jane's eyes.

"Jane, I'm sharing this with you as I would with a daughter, especially after hearing your part and what you are going through. I want to help you Jane, and you will soon know why," said Sharmila softly, holding Jane's hand. "My husband Ritesh," she continued "was born to a royal family in Southern India. The family received this painting as a gift from a Muslim King in the early nineteenth century. The Muslim king had to get rid of it for fear of his family being assassinated by fanatics. The King took his own life after giving away the painting."

"Ritesh's grandfather, who had promised the Muslim king to safeguard the painting, kept it in his reading room. The heavy painting could never be hung on a wall; it would always fall to the ground, and several people were tasked to hang it on the wall."

"One official finally came up with a better solution – he made a shallow recess in the wall for the painting to stand. I keep calling it a painting but it is actually a wooden handicraft studded with ivory, diamonds and precious stones that adorned the lady's dress," Sharmila paused, looking at Jane who was intently listening to her. "Have you read or heard the story behind the painting? Sorry, I'm assuming you did," said Sharmila.

"As a matter of fact, I have. I forgot to tell you that. I read a story on the internet about the young woman and her lover. It was the first time I read about the practice of *Sati*," Jane responded. "Please continue," she said to Sharmila not wanting to interrupt.

Sharmila continued, "Sati was a horrible practice followed in some parts of ancient India. Women were forced to enter the funeral pyre with their dead husbands, in the name of religion and for honor. It was a practice shocking to several parts of the world. The artwork was very controversial on account of the *Sati* aspect, even as it had a powerful story to tell - a story of love, honor and religion."

"Ritesh was just a newborn when his grandfather died of depression," continued Sharmila. "His grandfather used to spend hours in the night looking at the artwork. His only wish before death was to safeguard the artwork. Ritesh and I were distant cousins and we were engaged at a very young age, I got married to him when I was barely fourteen."

"Ritesh, his parents and I sailed to England in 1945. It was a time of intense freedom fights in India. We bought a beautiful place in London. Ritesh went to Medical School in Oxford, while I studied arts in Oxford," Sharmila paused to take a sip of her coffee and a bite of the Belgian waffle they had ordered.

Sharmila continued "You know, having led a very rich life as royals in India, it was difficult losing most of our assets, servants and comforts. Adjusting in London was tough, initially. We had brought along most of our precious jewels and ornaments. That included the *Sati Gita* artwork. We never opened it for several years; it was kept in a wooden safe box, specially made for it. The truth is that I had never seen it before."

Sharmila continued, "One day while we were out, my mother-in-law decided to take the artwork out of the box. As she was decorating the house, she kept it in our bedroom. Ritesh came back from school and looked at it for hours. He fell in love with the girl in the artwork. I have to say, she was very beautiful. Noticing his attraction to the painting and a little jealous, I moved it to the study room. I must admit that was a huge mistake - that was the last time Ritesh ever came back to the bedroom. He would spend hours staring at the painting. His father and he had repeated arguments about not focusing on studies and wasting time, staring at the painting."

"Ritesh soon made a decision to move to the United States, he applied for a transfer to Harvard Medical School and we moved to Boston. Within a year of our move, Ritesh's father died of depression, just like Ritesh's grandfather. We moved to Boston with our belongings. My mother-in-law and I hid the artwork in the basement. We lied to Ritesh that the painting was lost in transit."

Sharmila paused briefly, and continued, "Years passed, and everything went well. But my husband was never the same with me. He would spend all his time either studying, or at the hospital. Well, you know how a doctor's life is. One day when I was out shopping, Ritesh found the artwork. He was furious that we lied to him about the artwork. He kept the artwork in his study. That was the end of my peace of mind.

We had several fights and arguments about the artwork and why he was so mesmerized by it. When we learned through some of our contacts that the descendants of Richard Brooks were looking for the painting, I persuaded him every day to return it to them. He finally relented and we proceeded to Norwich in Norfolk, UK.

We met with a lady who was Richard Brooks' great-great-granddaughter, Anna. She believed that the artwork rightfully belonged to them and wanted it. Ritesh was not convinced. He decided not to give the painting to Anna," Sharmila paused briefly. She looked at Jane who did not take her eyes off Sharmila; Jane was listening to her with rapt attention.

Sharmila sipped some water and continued, "Ritesh started acting strangely after that and he even tried to kill me! That is when I fled to my brother here, who is a diamond merchant," tears rolled down her cheeks and Sharmila quickly wiped them away with a tissue. Sharmila leaned back and lamented, "Look at our lives; we were from a royal family and doing so well. Our lives were just torn apart by this artwork."

Jane reached across the table and touched Sharmila's hand. She said softly, "Sharmila, if you are not up to it, we can talk later."

Sharmila wiped her tears and said, "That's all right, Jane. I'd rather tell you the whole story now." She steeled herself and continued "About a year before Ritesh died, he gave the painting to Jeff, his very close friend at Harvard. Ritesh then came to Antwerp apologizing and begging me to return to Boston. I refused. He died a few months after meeting me."

She paused to take a deep breath and continued, "I must tell you Jane, Jeff will not give the artwork to you. After Ritesh's death I pleaded with him to give me the artwork so I could return it to the Brooks family. He gave me every excuse possible and never returned it. Did he tell you that his own son suffered addiction to the artwork, just like Ritesh, and died of a heart ailment at a very young age?"

Jane shook her head in shock, "No! Jeff did not mention that his son was dead."

Sharmila looked Jane in the eye and said with intense determination, "I want you to rob the painting and give it to the Brooks family. Please do it, I beg of you. You are the chosen one!" Jane was taken aback by the sudden plea from this dignified lady. She was speechless and barely nodded her head in confusion. They left the restaurant in silence. As they walked by the Brabo fountain, Sharmila asked, "Have you heard about the Brabo fountain?"

"No," replied Jane looking at the fountain that was lit from below creating sharp contrasts of light and shadow on the sculpture. It appeared to be a rather violent depiction of a man standing on a giant about to throw the giant's severed hand.

"That man is Silvius Brabo. He is standing on the evil giant Druoon Antigoon after slaying him. Brabo is throwing the giant's hand into the river *Scheldt*," explained Sharmila.

Jane stared at the sculpture, trying to interpret Sharmila's explanation and said, "That is gross; but the sculpture is incredible." They walked through the cobbled street lined by Flemish Renaissance buildings, to the parked car. They drove in silence to the Lindner Hotel, just around the block from where they had parked. Jane looked out at the storefronts and restaurants, lit beautifully at night.

Arriving at the hotel, Jane smiled at Sharmila and said, "Thank you so much for your time. It was a pleasure to meet somebody like you." She scribbled her e-mail address and number on a piece of paper and handed it to Sharmila. "Please send me the number for Anna Brooks."

Sharmila reached across her seat and hugged Jane. "You will hear from me soon," she said softly, "I wish I had a daughter like you."

As Sharmila drove off, Jane walked through the hotel doors to the elevator. She called her sister and talked to her about Sharmila and their conversation, she discussed her plan and how her sister can help her with this mission. She promised to keep Jen updated. "Hey Sis, I love you. Take care, and I will see you soon," said Jane.

Without wasting a moment, Jane opened her laptop and connected to the Internet. She checked her e-mail, and true to her word Sharmila had e-mailed the address and phone number for Anna Brooks. Jane made a reservation on Euro Rail from Antwerp to Brussels Midi, connecting to London St. Pancras. She browsed a little more and made another reservation at the St. Giles House Hotel in Norwich, England. She then called Swiss airlines and canceled her return trip to Boston. Exhausted and jetlagged, she kicked off her shoes and slumped on the bed.

Chapter 9

The sun shone directly on her face through the partially open blinds of the window. Jane woke up and looked at the clock on the nightstand. It was 10:30 am. She must have slept for almost twelve hours. She rose and walked to the hotel room window to open the blinds. The street below was bustling with traffic and pedestrians. She looked at the Cathedral of our Lady outlined in the brilliant morning sunshine and prayed, "Dear God, help me accomplish my mission".

She packed her bags and dressed hastily wanting to make it on time to catch the 2:00 pm train to Brussels. As she stepped off the elevator onto the lobby, her cell phone buzzed. It was an unknown number and she answered, "Hello, this is Jane."

"Hello Dear, this is Sharmila. I will pick you up; please tell me the time," Sharmila said chirpily. Jane said she would be ready in forty-five minutes. She checked out of the hotel and headed to the Hotel's restaurant for lunch.

After a quick lunch, Jane walked to the hotel lounge with her suitcase. She was just about to sit on the comfortable sofa when her cell phone rang again. Sharmila was at the hotel entrance and calling Jane from the car. Jane got into Sharmila's Mercedes and thanked her for the ride.

As they approached the station, Sharmila pulled to the curb and reached out for her handbag. She pulled out a small velvet pouch from her handbag and gave it to Jane. "What's this?" Jane asked, quite puzzled.

"These are the original precious stones from the artwork. They need to go back where they belong. I am entrusting them to you," Sharmila responded, placing the pouch in Jane's palm and firmly closing her fingers around it. She held Jane's closed hand for a while and Jane placed hers reassuringly on top of Sharmila's.

There was a moment of silence that bonded the women together. It seemed to give purpose to their undefined yet common desire to permanently bury the suffering and pain of generations. Jane tucked the pouch into her purse and said goodbye to Sharmila. She got her bags and walked to the main entrance of the train station. Jane turned back to catch a glimpse of Sharmila as she drove away.

Jane entered the beautiful nineteenth century Antwerp train station. She got her pass at the ticket counter and headed to her terminal to catch the train to Brussels. There was a connecting train to London, barely a few minutes after arrival at Brussels, and she managed to get on it. It was a long journey and she sat by the window, enjoying the beautiful landscape as she sipped her coffee and munched on a French croissant.

Arriving at St. Pancras International Station, Jane started looking around for directions, as she kept walking towards *The Meeting Place* sculpture. She gazed at the famous statue and looked away, blushing. Making room for the heavy pedestrian traffic at the station, she stepped closer to the statue and waited. Jane took out her cell phone from her bag when she heard her name being called out. She turned and saw her sister waving excitedly at her, pushing a cart with an outsized portfolio case and a small duffel bag.

Jane almost ran to her sister and hugged her tightly. Holding Jen's shoulder and looking into her eyes, she exclaimed, "Oh My God Jen, you did it!"

"Yes! It was a cakewalk. And the timing was perfect, as Jeff was away!" Jen said, barely able to contain her excitement. "I did exactly as you asked me to. I told the office assistant Dr. Stoker was having me fix mounts on the painting so he could hang it on the wall. She fell for it. I must have been pretty convincing, or she was pretty dumb. Can you believe I just wheeled the painting out of the office?"

Jen patted on the large case and said, "Gosh, it is heavy. I've padded it well with foam and clothes." Jen placed both hands on her sister's shoulders and said, "Jane, I wish I could hang out a bit, but I have a return flight from Heathrow in less than three hours." Jane wanted her to stay longer but knew that she could never make her sister change her mind.

Hugging her sister with tears in her eyes, she said, "Jen, I'm so thankful to you! I love you sis, I'm so lucky!"

Jen took her bag from the cart and walked away hurriedly. Jane hoisted her suitcase onto the cart and walked outside the bustling station. She found a hackney carriage right outside the station. She asked the driver to take her to a hardware store, where she purchased glue and a pair of forceps. They then drove to St. Giles Hotel in Norwich.

Chapter 10

St. Giles Hotel was an impressive boutique hotel and Jane was awed by the grandeur of the building and its beautiful surroundings. She checked into the hotel and walked up to her room waiting for her luggage. The bellboy wheeled it in shortly on a bell cart. She tipped him and quickly closed the door.

The room had classic furniture and there was an unmistakable old world English charm to it. Jane pulled out her laptop and sat on the cushioned desk chair. She looked up the location of Anna's residence online and tried to map the distance from her hotel. She wrote down Anna's phone number and address on the hotel stationery and put it in her purse.

Jane shut her laptop and rose from the chair. She opened the large case her sister brought over from Boston and carefully pulled out the artwork from the cover. She rested it against the bedroom wall and whispered, "You are going to be happy."

Jane picked up the hotel phone and dialed the number for Anna Brooks. "Hello" a male voice responded. Jane took a deep breath, "Hi, I am Jane Reynolds from Boston. I would like to speak to Anna Brooks. Is she there?"

After a pause, she heard him, "Could you please hold Ma'm?" Jane waited as she heard distant voices and a woman came on the phone. "Hello, this is Anna."

"Hi Miss Brooks, I am Jane Reynolds from Boston. I'm visiting Norwich and would like to meet with you if you can spare the time. This is about..."

Anna interrupted, "Sure, I would love to meet you, Jane! Sharmila called and talked about you. I'm very glad you are here in Norwich. It's rather late today; can we meet tomorrow morning at ten? I live very close to the Norwich Cathedral! Do you need directions?" Anna spoke crisply but with heavily accented English.

"Sure, ten in the morning will be perfect, I can get some rest. I do have the directions to your house," Jane answered. She wished Anna good night and hung up.

Jane took out the pouch given to her by Sharmila, and gently laid out the precious stones on the desk. She opened the portfolio case again and placed the artwork on the floor. She carefully set about replacing the imitation stones on the artwork with the original precious stones. She painstakingly pried out one stone at a time, and inserted a matching original in its place with a tiny dab of glue.

When she was done, Jane held the artwork against the light and was quite thrilled to see the stones glitter in the light.

She admired the artwork for some time and carefully covered it with a cloth. She turned in for the night after setting the alarm. Jane knew she would have a busy day.

Chapter 11

Jane woke up startled as the alarm rang shrilly. She called the front desk asking to arrange a taxicab for her. It had snowed in the night and Jane dressed in jeans, boots and a snow jacket. After taking one long look at the artwork, she packed it in the case and hurried down to her waiting cab.

"The house is on Quay Side near Fye Bridge," Jane told the driver as she handed him a paper with the address. Nodding his head, he drove slowly through the beautiful streets dusted with powdery snow. The driver looked at the rear view mirror and asked, "Is this your first visit to Norwich, Ma'm?"

"Yes."

"I will drive you through the Norwich Cathedral then," the driver said cheerfully.

As they drove through Exchange Street and Queen Street, Jane took in the neatness of the streets and the charming houses that lined them. The driver slowed down at Palace Street so Jane could view the Cathedral as they drove by. They continued to Quay Side and the car stopped near a brick row house with wrought iron window planters. Thanking and paying the taxi driver who helped her with the suitcase, Jane stepped up to the door. She rang the doorbell and waited.

A plump woman opened the door and greeted Jane. She led her into the living room to wait for Anna. Jane sat on the couch, looking at the small black and white photographs that almost entirely covered the walls. Presently, a lady in her mid sixties walked in and smiled warmly at Jane, who stood up and smiled back.

"Hello Jane, I'm Anna" she said and welcomed her with a warm hug. "Those are photographs of my parents and grandparents; and some lithographs of our ancestors."

"Quite a collection you have here," commented Jane, sitting down.

"Thank you so much for coming all the way from Antwerp. Sharmila talked a lot about you," said Anna looking at Jane.

"No problem at all, my mission is now accomplished!" Jane said, elated. "Here is the artwork," she pointed to the suitcase leaning against the wall, "Where does it go now?"

Anna smiled at Jane "Do you know we have been searching for this artwork for more than seventy five years? Researching this artwork, my great grandfather went to India looking for it, but in vain. I was awfully close to getting it from Ritesh; he just walked away after talking to me. I had given up hope; and here you are, and my hope is back," Anna exclaimed, visibly elated.

"I do want to know where the artwork is headed, Anna" Jane insisted, looking into Anna's eyes.

Anna rose from the couch and walked to the suitcase. She looked down at the case and looked up at Jane, "Back to where it belongs. It will be broken into pieces and buried near the Soane River in Bihar, India." Anna looked down at the case again and continued, "I am leaving this evening. I have already booked my tickets. I will not open this case as I have been asked not to look at it," she said with a distinct finality. Jane stood up and asked, "When will I know?"

"Soon!" responded Anna. Jane bid her farewell and declined a ride. She realized her hotel was not that far and she wanted to walk back. Besides, she memorized the way on her short taxi ride to Anna's house.

Jane stepped out of Anna's house and started walking towards Fye Bridge, smiling to herself. The frosty morning didn't bother her. She stopped at the bridge to look at the willow trees and leaned on the bridge, looking at the water below. She stared at the frozen water, at an image of a beautiful Indian lady - the lady in the artwork. She was dressed in a flowing blue skirt and blouse, with her mid rib exposed and a veil covering her long black hair. She was walking towards a sleeping young girl and waking her up saying *"Agni, Agni!"* The girl wakes up and runs down the stairs to see the kitchen on fire and yells "Fire! Mom, Dad, wake up!" The family runs out of the house as it burns down to ashes. Jane sees the Indian lady smile at her as she walks away towards a large banyan tree.

This vision was certainly not like the disturbing ones Jane had been experiencing before. She stood staring at the water for a while; then walked away from the bridge towards the Norwich

Cathedral. She felt as if a veil of confusion and sorrow had just been lifted. As she approached the Cathedral, she looked up at the sky as snowflakes starting falling on her face. She smiled with joy, as a great sense of accomplishment washed over her being.

Chapter 12

Opening the door, Jane entered her Boston apartment, pulling her bags inside. She closed the door and walked to her phone to check messages. "Jane! Call me when you get back. Your cell phone seemed to be switched off!" It was her sister.

Jane called her sister and reached her answering machine. She left a message, "Hey there, I missed you guys. I just got back. I decided to stay back one more day in Norwich; took a tour of London and enjoyed my time. Talk to you soon. I love you, Sis!! Thank you so much."

Jane walked into her bedroom and turned on her laptop. She opened the bookmarked web page *Controversial 1783 Painting by Richard Brooks* and carefully read the story again. Every word was the same till she reached a paragraph in the physician's narration of the story to Richard Brooks. It was different and she started reading intently.

Heartbroken, Ismail made several attempts to save the love of his life from the miserable marriage. The Nawab learned of his son's situation and sent him abroad on a religious mission. When Ismail returned after three years, he still could not forget

Gita. He secretly sent her a note asking her to meet him. Gita agreed to meet her true love. On the very same day that Gita was to secretly meet Ismail at night, her husband died of old age and ailments. His last words to his wife were, "You are free now."

At nightfall, Gita sneaked out of her home and with the help of her trusted maids, made her way to the temple. She waited for her lover under the banyan tree, while her three maids spread out and stood guard. With tears in her eyes, Gita sat on a small rock under the banyan tree, fully dressed as a bride and adorned in wedding jewelry. After a short while, Ismail came to the riverbank. He stopped upon seeing her, moved to tears by the sight of his beloved after these years of separation and mesmerized by her beauty.

He knelt before Gita and professed his unending love for her. He swore that he would take her away from her misery and begged her to come away with him. Gita looked at Ismail and cried. They hugged and cried for joy, holding onto each other and never wanting to let go. Ismail and Gita eloped that night and lived a happy married life. When she died at an old age, Ismail memorialized his beloved with the artwork that captured her beautiful face in the moment on that fateful night that was forever etched in his soul.

Jane scrolled to the bottom of the page and saw the picture of the artwork on the website. The beautiful bride Gita was decked in jewelry and seated under the banyan tree, smiling with expectant joy. Slowly Jane's eyes moved to the bottom left of the painting where the inscription read "*Gita, the Happy Bride*". On the bottom right, it still read "Richard Brooks Year 1783". Jane smiled and walked to the window. She looked down at the street and the people below, still smiling.

Seven Days with Miljana

Chapter 1

Suwei looked out of the window at the crowded streets of Tai Po. The city was aglow with the orange wash of the setting sun. She squinted up at the sun that was about to disappear behind the mass of buildings. She looked down at the street again, hoping to see her daughter return home from the farewell lunch party her daughter's friends were throwing for her. She grew anxious with each passing minute and kept glancing at the clock. The doorbell rang and Suwei rushed to open the door. She was relieved as her teenage daughter Lin, walked in and slumped on the couch.

"Dui bu qi' Mama, I'm late, I tried my best to get home early," she said. "There were so many friends who came to the lunch and were very sad to see me go." Lin set her bag down and pulled out the gifts from her friends, to show her mother.

Sitting next to her daughter, Suwei could see that Lin was feeling the pain of having to leave her friends behind. She said caringly "Lin, Australia is a beautiful place, you are going to enjoy studying there. You are going to make new friends, from different cultures and backgrounds," she paused for a moment and continued, "Your Uncle called me this morning. He said your tuition has been paid and your classes are starting mid-February. I've packed all we need to take. Aunt Wei-Wei will take care of the house for us, while we are in Australia."

Suwei slowly released her daughter's hand and walked towards the window. Not hearing Lin say anything, Suwei turned to her and continued softly, "Lin, we don't have much left here. Hong Kong is not the same anymore. This is 1999, almost two years since China took over. Things have changed. So much more is going to change. I'm filled with your father's memories and a change of place will help us get over our grief." Suwei quickly turned back to the window, wiping her tears. Lin walked up to her mother and leaned on her, wrapping her arms around her.

After her father's passing away, the two had come to draw solace in each other's company. His being away on military duty while alive had already bonded the two. After her husband's death, Suwei had come to rely on her daughter for companionship. She kept herself engaged throughout the day in chores and dreaded being alone with nothing left to do.

Suwei walked to the kitchen and filled noodle soup in two white china bowls. She returned to the living room and set the bowls on the coffee table. They sipped the hot soup in silence and decided to go for a stroll. They walked down the stairs of their apartment complex to the busy street below. Holding Lin's hand, Suwei said excitedly, "Let's go to *Man Mo* Temple and pray for your success. I want you to study well and have a successful career! Your father always dreamed of you managing several people and working in a high-rise building with your own office!" she smiled at Lin who was smiling too.

They stopped to meet some old friends on the way, and bid them farewell. Suwei and Lin soon reached the temple and walked through the wooden doors, into the smoke-filled hall with spiral incense coils hanging from the ceiling. They lit incense sticks and knelt down to pray to *Man Tai*, the Literature God.

As Suwei prayed, she was reminded of her husband and how she had prayed for him every single day that he was away from home. She prayed now for strength and her daughter's future. Tears flowed from her eyes as she bowed down to pray. Lin touched her mother reassuringly and smiled. "Mama, I will do well. Don't worry about me."

It was late in the evening and they walked back home through the moonlit streets of Tai Po in silence. They packed and made travel preparations for the next day. Chants of *Om tare tuttare ture mama ayur punye jnyana pushtim kuru ye soha* played in the background. They were both tense about the next day's journey and it was late before they could finally sleep.

Chapter 2

Suwei awoke to the hustle and bustle in the street below. She walked to Lin's bed and gently touching her daughter's head, whispered in her ear, "Wake up Lin, today is a new start." Aunt Wei-Wei arrived early in the morning to help Suwei and Lin with their last minute packing and errands. As they got ready to take the cab to the airport, Suwei called her brother in Melbourne and confirmed the time she and Lin would be arriving at the airport.

Handing over the house keys to Wei Wei, Suwei hugged her cousin and thanked her for offering to watch the house for them. Suwei and Lin stepped out to the waiting cab. As they rode to Chek Lap Kok Airport, they looked back at the house where they had spent so many years of their lives.

When they arrived at the airport, Lin looked around and memories rushed to her mind. "Mama, we saw Dad for the last time here."

Suwei grabbed her daughter's hand and said, "Let's go, we can't be late," trying to quickly distract her daughter. They boarded the Cathay Pacific flight to Melbourne.

Soon Lin was sleeping with her head resting on Suwei's shoulder. Suwei thought about her hometown, Lantau Island, where she grew up as a child. Her parents worked at the Buddhist monastery. She had met her husband at the monastery. She reminisced about their joyful days when Lin was born and grew up as a toddler. Memories of her husband in army fatigues, bidding them farewell at the airport brought tears to her eyes. Wiping her tears, Suwei silently chanted prayers and tried to get some sleep.

"Good afternoon, Ladies and Gentlemen! This is captain Jim Walters. I hope you had a pleasant flight. We'll be arriving in Melbourne in approximately 20 minutes. The temperature is 23 degrees Celsius with light rain. Please fasten your seat belts and remain seated," the flight captain announced, awakening Suwei and Lin, who looked out of the window in excitement, marveling at the aerial view of the city of Melbourne.

After the plane landed, Lin and Suwei collected their bags, went through immigration and walked out of the arrival gate. Lin spotted her Uncle at a distance and ran to him calling out "*Shūshu*". Suwei's brother Yen was a short young man with a pleasant demeanor and thoughtful eyes. He had not seen his sister and niece for a long time and had eagerly awaited their arrival. After numerous phone discussions, he had succeeded in convincing Suwei to move to Melbourne and let Lin pursue her schooling in Australia. He hugged his favorite niece and turned to Suwei who was wheeling the luggage. "Finally you two made it! I'm so glad to see you *Jie jie!* And I missed you so much, Lin."

Suwei and Lin followed Yen to the parking lot. "Nice car, Yen. Is this the car you were talking about last year?"

"Yes! Holden Commodore VT S! It's a cool Australian car. I love it!" replied a beaming Yen as he placed their bags in the trunk. They drove out of the airport onto State Route 43. Suwei and Lin looked out of the window at the sights of the city. Suwei had so many questions to ask Yen, about his life in Melbourne and how he had managed to live alone all these years.

"So, are you dating anybody, or are you still following our *Shūshu's* footsteps?" Suwei wondered often about their Uncle's influence on Yan. Their Uncle, *Shūshu*, had been a staunch Buddhist and had chosen to live the life of a hermit for most of his life. "Hard to believe you did not find someone here or fall in love" Suwei probed her brother.

"*Jie jie*, I'm thirty-nine years old. Who will marry me? Moreover, my devotion to Lord Buddha is very strong. I want to remain single and spend my late years in a Monastery. I know you and Mama disagreed with my views, but I hope you understand," responded Yen, looking at his sister in the rear view mirror. Lin, who was sitting in the front passenger seat, turned around and smiled at her mother who couldn't hide her expression of disagreement.

"That's the Bolte Bridge, over there." exclaimed Yen, pointing out to them the imposing bridge spanning the Yarra River. He talked about the New Year eve celebration at Yarra River and his visit to the Melbourne Cricket Grounds. He promised to show them all the best sights in Melbourne.

After a forty-five minute ride from the airport to Clayton, they pulled up the driveway of Yen's one-storey suburban house. Yen got out of the car and opened the door for his sister. He said excitedly in Chinese, "Welcome Sister! I wanted you to attend the house warming, but I'm glad you're with me now."

Suwei stepped out from the car, patted his shoulder affectionately and said, "Lovely house, Yen. I'm sure you are a successful professor and doing very well. I'm happy you moved to Melbourne."

Suwei and Lin followed Yen across the front yard that had a neat garden of roses and several flowering shrubs around the lawn. "Mama, look at that on the tree! Is that a koala, *Shūshu*?" Lin exclaimed, pointing at the street tree fronting the lawn.

"It's a wombat, look closely and you will see her carrying the baby wombat!" Yen said. He opened the trunk and carried the bags into the house. Suwei followed her brother, calling out to Lin to come inside the house.

The entry was dominated by a huge bronze Buddha statue. Two bronze elephants flanked the Buddha and everything in the hallway looked spotless. The house was filled with indoor plants and paintings of the Buddha.

"*Wa sei!*" exclaimed Lin as she took in the neatness and tasteful décor of the house. "*Shūshu*, your house is very beautiful!" For a man who had limited wants and had chosen to give up many of life's luxuries, the house looked surprisingly well decorated.

"It's yours too, Lin" responded Yen warmly to his niece. He walked to the kitchen, eager to show Suwei the house. As Suwei admired the backyard, Yen said to her, "You can plant whatever you want, the backyard is all yours! As you can see, there is a lot of space for gardening in the backyard." Yen showed them their bedrooms, his own small bedroom and a fourth bedroom that was converted to a meditation room.

At dinner, Yen enquired Suwei about their relatives and friends in Hong Kong, and they talked about the changes the country went through in two years, after it was handed over to the Chinese Government. "Lin was finding it difficult in school, some teachers stopped speaking English and were forcing students to converse in Cantonese," said Suwei.

"Well, we are in Melbourne now. She has a different challenge to face," continued Suwei, looking at Lin.

"Monday is February 22nd, Lin, you need to complete your University orientation," Yen reminded his niece. "I will be there to help you with the enrolment before I go to the Caulfield campus for a meeting."

"I'm excited and scared," said Lin, "I will have one day to rest!" she sighed and yawned sleepily.

After kissing her daughter good night, Suwei walked to Yen's bedroom and sat on his bed. Yen was reading a book. Suwei said softly "I wish I had convinced him to quit the army and come to Melbourne. I badly wanted him to quit the army and take up the job you found for him."

"Your husband was a stubborn man, he did not believe in peace," Yin sighed and continued, "Don't worry about the past; it is too late now to think of the past. Lin is going to have a wonderful future. You go ahead and get a good night's sleep." Thanking her brother for everything, Suwei turned in for the night.

Chapter 3

Yen, Suwei and Lin set out early in the day to visit the Buddhist Society in Yuroke. The journey from Clayton to Yuroke lasted about an hour and they laughed and chatted on the way. It was a beautiful sunny day with a gentle breeze, and they spent some time in peaceful meditation at the Tibetan Temple. While Yen was busy doing volunteer work, Lin and Suwei toured the rose garden, admiring the variety of roses and flowers and enjoying the fragrance in the air.

On the way back, they parked their car in Central Melbourne and walked along the Yarra River, enjoying ice cream, talking and joking. Suwei looked at her daughter's happy face and turned to her brother with a thankful expression in her eyes. They then visited the Clayton campus of Monash University where Lin would be starting her studies the coming week. They toured the campus grounds, visiting the Sports and Recreation center, the Alexander Theatre, and the Museum of Arts and Science Center. Yen showed them the building where he worked. "This is your pre-tour, Lin! Did you like it so far?" asked Yen.

"Yes *Shūshu,* I love it!" Suwei was equally excited, "I love this

University! It has so many facilities! Lin, you are so lucky that *Shūshu* is a Professor on this same campus! You will not feel alone, till you make new friends."

Suwei woke up early the next day to prepare breakfast and pack lunch for Yen and Lin. After they left for school, she watered the plants, made the beds and rearranged the bedroom closets. She spent the remainder of the afternoon reading a book and awaited their return. When Suwei heard the car pull into the driveway, she quickly opened the front door. Realizing that they had stopped for groceries on the way, she rushed out to help them with the grocery bags. Suwei asked her daughter, "Did everything go well at school?"

"Yes, Mama, I liked the orientation, the classes start very soon. I will be going everyday with *Shūshu* in the morning and returning home with him so I don't have to take the bus; at least till I get familiar with the place," Lin responded.

"Oh, and she made some new friends today!" Yen said to Lin excitedly, as he walked into the house with the last of the grocery bags. "Lin, do you want to tell me about your new friends?" Suwei asked. "Not now Mama, I'm so tired. We can talk tomorrow," responded Lin impatiently. Suwei understood that they were both tired and served them an early dinner.

Yen was watching the popular Seven Nightly News. Suwei had finished her chores and came into the living room. She sat next to her brother with a book. Lin was reading in her room. "That's John Howard, Australia's Prime Minister," said Yen.

"Oh! As you can see, I am not very interested in politics. I know almost nothing about politics," Suwei said, looking at the TV. Shortly thereafter, Yen wished her good night and retired to his room, saying he had an early lecture and that they were starting early the next day. Suwei turned off the lights and went to her bedroom. She lay on the bed and stared at the ceiling; thinking of her home in Tai Po, her friends and relatives.

As the days passed, Lin was spending more time at the University, working on her assignments at the campus. When she was home, Lin was either studying or talking to her new friends on the phone. Yen too was extremely busy with his work at the University and had to pick Lin up before heading home. They often returned late and were too exhausted to chat with Suwei.

Suwei felt neglected by her daughter and was beginning to feel quite lonely in the house. She eagerly awaited her daughter's return, even if Lin seemed indifferent or too tired to chat. When Suwei tried to converse with Lin, she was almost always evading her mother on the pretext of having a lot of studying to do for the next day's class.

When this started to become a regular pattern, Suwei became very worried about her daughter's transformation. She approached Yen one evening when he was watching the television news. "Yen, I have noticed a lot of change in Lin, she does not talk to me like before. I'm getting worried," said Lin.

"She's fine; she is going through so many changes - new friends, new commitments. The load of assignments and tests can get to them, you know. She will be back to normal during the summer break. Let's give her some time and space," Yen reassured her. He returned to watching the news on the television.

He seemed increasingly agitated with the war footage on TV that was being broadcast repetitively. "War…War…War! I'm tired of watching this disgusting news about the conflicts in Bosnia and Kosovo. Day after day, the news is about the suffering there – Bosnia, Serbia, Yugoslavia, Kosovo –there is no end in sight. Why can't people live in peace!" he lamented, standing up.

After a few moments, he regained his composure and walked slowly to the meditation room. Not quite understanding what Yen was grumbling about, Suwei went to the kitchen to finish her chores. She thought this was not the best time to fret and burden her brother with her worries.

Chapter 4 - Day 1

One day, Suwei had finished all the chores early and had finished watering the plants. Everything seemed an unending routine to her now, and she was always running out of things to do. Soon, the boredom overtook her and she decided to walk to the nearby supermarket. Taking a foldable cart with her, Suwei set out on a stroll to the supermarket. A gentle breeze was blowing and the sky was bright with a few passing clouds. She stopped by a Chinese grocery store first to pick up some vegetables and condiments and continued on towards the Supermarket.

Oddly, the supermarket appeared very crowded for a weekday afternoon. Suwei finished the grocery shopping and proceeded to the line at the counter. As she was placing the items on the counter, Suwei noticed a beautiful young girl with long brown hair and light brown eyes right behind her. The girl smiled at her and Suwei smiled back.

She finished paying at the counter and stepped aside to transfer the items to her personal cart. As she was arranging the bags to fit in her little cart, an accented voice from behind asked her, "Do you need any help?" It was the same girl who was standing behind her at the counter.

"No I'm all set, but thank you," replied Suwei politely. "Are you Lin Wang's mother?" asked the girl. "Yes!" responded Suwei quite alarmed, "How do you know?"

"I go to the same class as Lin for Political Science," the girl replied in her Eastern European accent. "My name is Miljana," she said holding out her slender hand. Excited to learn that she knew her daughter, Suwei shook her hand warmly. "Did you drive to this place? If not, I can drive you back to your place. I have a car," Miljana gushed excitedly.

"Hmm...Mm" Suwei hesitated, looking at her overloaded cart. "Sure, if it's not a trouble," she added quickly.

Suwei wheeled her cart across the parking lot with Miljana. "Where do you live, Miljana?"

"I live in Brunswick, with my Uncle. I come to Clayton once a week. Sorry, its' an old car," Miljana said, gesturing embarrassingly at an old Honda Civic. She helped Suwei load her groceries and foldable cart in the trunk. They got in the car and Suwei tried to give her the directions.

"Lin has never talked about you? Do you know her well?" asked Suwei quite puzzled, unable to recollect her daughter mentioning Miljana's name. "We have met once, maybe twice. I like Lin. She speaks good English. You too speak good English," Miljana said, again in a heavy accent. "We are from Hong Kong. I used to teach English at a school for several years! Where are you from?" asked Suwei.

"I am from Yugoslavia," Miljana said. As Miljana drove with relative ease, Suwei guessed her age to be around eighteen or nineteen. Her brown wavy hair almost reached her waist while seated. She had a slim figure with a smooth and fair skin tone. Up close, Suwei thought she looked very beautiful. Miljana turned towards Suwei and asked with a smile, "Can I call you Nënë? In my language, it means mother."

"Sure, you can, dear!" responded Suwei warmly. She was already feeling quite comfortable with Miljana. She showed her the street turns as they neared home. When they reached home, Suwei invited her in for a cup of Chinese tea.

Miljana seemed very excited to spend time with her. She helped Suwei bring in the groceries. Seeing Suwei take off her shoes before entering the house, Miljana took hers off at the door. "Wow!" she exclaimed, entering the living room, "This house is so beautiful. It is like a Buddhist temple!"

Suwei smiled, "Thank you! I can't take credit for this, its' my brother's house. We are just guests here." Suwei took the rest of the grocery bags into the kitchen, "Let me make some tea for us."

While Suwei was brewing the tea, Miljana walked around, admiring the decorative works of art in the living room. "Is this your brother and you when you where small?!" exclaimed Miljana when she caught sight of a black and white photograph in an ornate picture frame. "Small?" Suwei lifted her eyebrows jokingly at Miljana. She smiled and corrected herself, "I mean young. Sorry, my English is not very good."

Suwei returned with the hot green tea and cookies and they

sat at the dining table. Suwei asked, "Miljana, where did you say you came from?"

"Yugoslavia. Actually, I grew-up in Pristina and lived in Belgrade for a few years. My mother is from Kosovo and my father is from Serbia…" Noticing Suwei's puzzled look, she stopped. "I think you don't know where these places are, Nënë." Suwei rose and quickly walked into her bedroom. She returned with an atlas of the world. Miljana showed her where Serbia and Kosovo were located and told her about the war there.

Suwei refilled Miljana's cup with green tea and asked, "How did you come to Australia?" "You know about the war in Yugoslavia, Nënë?" Miljana asked, pulling her long hair backwards and tying it into a knot. Suwei said she didn't and that she hardly watched the news. Miljana continued to talk, "I was born in Pristina, my mother was Albanian and my father was Serb. They met in Pristina University and got married. Their parents opposed the marriage," she said with much sadness in her voice. Suwei listened with rapt attention.

"My parents were very happy. They had five children, and I am the fourth. I have two older sisters, one older brother and a younger brother," she said. "My parents were both professors at Pristina University. Around 1985, both lost their jobs. So my father went to Belgrade and found work in Belgrade University. My mother remained in Pristina." Miljana paused, with her eyes focused on the cup of tea. As she sipped the tea, Suwei asked "Where were you, Miljana?"

"I went with my father, and my little brother came with me. I wish I had never left my mother and sisters," she said, with tears rolling down her cheeks. "All that fighting and bombing…people dying," she started sobbing.

Suwei got up from her chair and walked to Miljana's side. Putting a comforting hand on her shoulder, she said "I'm sorry. Let us not talk about this now. You are a happy young girl."

"Nënë, I came here two years ago and I'm living with my Uncle – my father's cousin and his wife. They don't treat me well. They hate my mother as she was an Albanian." Miljana looked at Suwei and asked hesitantly, "Can I see you again and talk to you?"

"Sure, Dear. You can come here anytime; I'm alone at home during the day." Miljana's face lit up. "Thank you," she said. Looking at her wristwatch, she jumped up. "I have to go now, I'm so glad I met you. You have such a pleasant face; it brings a lot of peace to my mind. Can I take your number to call you?"

Taking Suwei's phone number, Miljana rushed to her car. Suwei stood at the front door and looked at the car as Miljana sped away. Suwei was saddened by Miljana's words, but she was happy to have met a new friend. "What a different person! The world is indeed an amazing place!" she thought.

She was about to close the door, when her brother's car drove into the driveway. Lin and Yen, walked into the house, tired as usual. Suwei realized with a start that she had forgotten to cook for them. She rushed to the kitchen to prepare a quick dinner. "I'm hungry, Mama. Why is the food not ready yet?" whined Lin in frustration. "I'm sorry, Honey. I had a guest at home - she is from your school. I think you know her!"

said Suwei, excited to share the news of her meeting with Miljana.

"A guest?" asked Lin, sitting next to her Uncle on the couch. He had switched on the television to his usual news channel. "Yes, she said she attended Political Science class with you. Her name is Miljana, a very pretty girl," said Suwei, bringing two cups of tea for Lin and Yen. "I don't know anybody by that name," said Lin with a frown. She couldn't recollect meeting anyone by that name at school.

"She seems to be a nice girl Lin, you should talk to her."

"Mama, I told you I don't know any such person," Lin said rather impatiently. "Whatever…" she muttered and walked away to her bedroom "Call me when the food is ready."

Suwei was upset and embarrassed with her daughter's behavior and turned to her brother, who waved his hand dismissively, "Just let it go! She is meeting people from various cultures and seeing different faces. I think she is upset because you called the girl pretty. Give her some space." Lin resumed watching the news. Suwei saw the merit in what her brother just said and tried to calm down. She returned to the kitchen to finish cooking their dinner, still thinking about her daughter's outburst.

Chapter 5 - Day 2

It was exactly a week after Suwei had met Miljana. Suwei was hanging out the clothes to dry in the backyard. She was thinking about Miljana and their meeting, when the doorbell rang. She hoped it was Miljana. Suwei rushed to the front door expectantly and was delighted to see Miljana.

Miljana hugged Suwei warmly and said, "I got some cake for you, I made it last night." She walked into the house remembering to remove her shoes at the door. Suwei was very excited and happy at her arrival. She went to the kitchen to place the cake on a plate. "I also got a music cassette from a friend. Do you have a stereo?" she asked. Suwei went to her daughter's room and returned with a portable stereo player.

Miljana was wearing a blue skirt smocked at the waist and a white t-shirt, the same dress she wore a week ago when Suwei met her for the first time. Suwei placed the stereo on the coffee table and went to the kitchen to get some tea to go with the cake. Miljana put the cassette in the player and started singing with the song, Mambo Number 5. "One, two, three, four, five," she sang and danced heartily.

When Suwei walked into the room and placed the tray with tea and cake on the coffee table, Miljana grabbed her arm and pleaded with her to dance. Suwei hesitated, but gave in to her persuasion. She danced with Miljana, giggling and laughing at her own moves. "Take one step left, one step right…" Miljana sang along with the stereo player, in her Serbian accent.

Both danced to the song and fell on the carpet, laughing. Suwei sat up and looked at Miljana who was lying on the floor and said, "That was so much fun, Miljana. I have not laughed so much in several months." She leaned down and kissed Miljana on her forehead. Miljana rose up giggling and said, "I used to dance a lot with my mother. We used to play Albanian music and dance for hours. She was a professor of religious studies, and a PhD." Miljana paused and asked Suwei who was listening intently to her, "Is it OK if I talk about myself? I need someone to talk to…"

"Of course you can. Please be free to talk to me anytime, Miljana." Suwei told her emphatically.

Sitting up and taking a piece of the cake, she said, "Nënë, you know, my father never talked to my mother after he lost his job. He thought he lost his job because he was a Serb. He started hating Albanians. We suffered a lot as a family, because my mother was Albanian and my father was a Serb," she paused and struggled to find the right words, "We were so happy before he lost his job. Once that happened, he would shout at us and treat us badly. My mother worked so hard to keep the family together. One day my father asked us to choose either him or mother - none of us wanted to go with him…" She stopped and stared at the wall, finding it difficult to go on, yet wanting to tell Suwei so much about the hurt that was bundled up inside her.

Suwei asked, "Why did you go with him, then?"

"My Nënë asked me to go. She was worried that nobody would take care of him," Miljana responded. "So I left for Belgrade with my father and younger brother. We were treated very badly by other people when they learned that my mother was Albanian. My brother was beaten in school every day."

"We would visit our mother and sisters every three months," she continued. "My mother made the best *sarma* and *proja!*" she said.

"What is that?" Suwei asked, noticing Miljana smile as she fondly remembered her mother.

"Sarma are rolls made of sauerkraut and proja is bread of corn."

"Oh, you mean corn bread," Suwei said. "Where did you learn to speak English, Miljana?"

"My sisters and I went to a school where English was a second language, so we learned English and watched some Hollywood movies," Miljana said laughing. "I have watched Jackie Chan movies, dubbed in Serbian too!"

Suwei was surprised, "Really? I did not know Jackie Chan was popular in Yugoslavia!!"

They continued chatting as Miljana followed Suwei to the back yard to fold the clothes. Miljana ran behind a butterfly trying to catch it. Suwei marveled at her youthful spirit that hid so much pain within. She was happy to see Miljana laugh heartily.

Miljana looked at her watch and told Suwei she had to rush home before her Uncle and Aunt returned from work. She hugged Suwei thanking her for her time, and left hurriedly.

Even though she promised to come the following week and talk more about her life events, Suwei stood in the doorway and watched Miljana drive away with a heavy heart. "I have met her only twice and yet, I feel my daughter is going away. Why do I feel that way? I hope I will see her soon," thought Suwei, feeling a sudden emptiness when Miljana departed.

Chapter 6 - Day 3

A week passed, Suwei eagerly waited for Miljana to visit her. It was a Thursday afternoon, and Suwei was having her lunch, when the phone bell rang. She ran to the phone and was rather disappointed to hear a telemarketer. Just as she hung up, she heard the door bell. She opened the door and was shocked to see a sweating Miljana at the door with a badly bruised and bleeding knee.

Suwei helped her into the living room and ran to get the first aid kit asking Miljana what happened and how she got hurt. Suwei had noticed that Miljana did not come in her car.

She looked worriedly at Miljana, who was wearing the same blue skirt and white t-shirt as the last time they met. Watching Suwei as she gently cleaned and dressed the wound, Miljana said hesitantly, "My Uncle took away my car. He did not want me to drive anymore. I came walking, when a dog chased me and I fell down. I screamed at it and it left me alone."

Suwei looked at her perplexed. "Why did your Uncle take your car away? Why would he do that?" Suwei asked.

Miljana continued to stare at the wound and said, "I came here to my uncle's house because I couldn't live in Yugoslavia. My Uncle is married to an Australian and they both treat me very badly. They don't let me study or go to school. I have missed a lot of classes," she stopped and sobbed. Suwei sat next to Miljana and held her close. "Why can't you go back, or find some work here?"

"Where do I go? I'm on a student visa and I have nowhere to go?" she cried.

Still holding her comfortingly, Suwei asked, "Why don't you go back to your mother?"

"I can't, she is not alive" Miljana continued to cry. Suwei was shocked and speechless when she heard that. She held Miljana close to her and let her calm down. Miljana wiped her tears and said, "You know Nënë, war is not easy. Life changes completely," and she started sobbing uncontrollably.

Suwei quickly got a box of tissues and wiped Miljana's eyes. "Please don't cry, dear. I'm sorry I asked you so many questions. Everything is going to be alright. Come with me to the meditation room," she said. Suwei led Miljana to the meditation room. It had a statue of Buddha and pictures of Buddha on the wall. "Let's pray to God for peace and happiness," she said and knelt on the floor. Miljana knelt awkwardly on her good leg, and they were both quiet for some time.

Miljana stopped crying and looked at Buddha's statue. She tried to regain her composure and forced a smile as she choked with emotion. "My mother used to get bonus money in the summers and she used to take us to a place called *Pejë*. We used to swim in the Drini River. It was always only the four of us - my sisters, my mother and I," she paused. "Those were my most memorable days!" she reminisced with a twinkle in her teary eyes.

"I see her in you, Nënë!" Miljana smiled and looked at Suwei. Suwei was moved to tears. She looked at Miljana lovingly and listened. "It is amazing, I'm from Kosovo and you are from Hong Kong, I feel so comfortable with you," said Miljana. Suwei turned towards the Buddha statue and said, "We are all one race Miljana, the human race!"

Nodding her head in acknowledgment, Miljana squatted on the floor close to the wall as she held her wounded leg with both hands. "My mother was sick one day, when I was in Belgrade with my father. There was a lot of bombing in Belgrade, so we were hiding in a temporary shelter. My sister tried to call us. She tried so hard to reach us," recollected Miljana, leaning her back to the wall and looking up at the ceiling. "My oldest sister, Mirjeta left my mother and my other sister at home and went to get medicine for my mother and she never came back," she stopped, unable to go on.

Suwei looked at Miljana and said, "Dear, you have to stop now. This will make you feel more depressed. Let me get you something to eat."

"No, I have to go. I have to buy eggs for my Uncle. I need to cook before they return home," said Miljana, standing up and limping towards the front door.

At the door Miljana turned to Suwei and tapped her bandaged wound. "Thank you for everything!" she said and smiled. "Next week, I will try to bring my Uncle's car, I will convince them. I will take you to Melbourne, and we can go shopping!" she exclaimed cheerfully.

Suwei touched Miljana's head and hugged her. "Sure, let's have fun! I want to see you happy." On the driveway, Miljana stopped and showed Suwei a wombat on the tree, carrying her young one on her back. The wombats were staring at them. She walked away, limping slightly.

After Miljana left, Suwei felt the same depression she felt when Miljana left the previous week, only this time the pining was stronger and she was very concerned about Miljana's life with her relatives.

She went to the meditation room and prayed. "The poor girl is suffering so much! My problems are nothing in comparison. God give her the strength," she prayed fervently for Miljana.

In the evening, when her brother and daughter were home, Suwei told them that Miljana had visited her. Lin did not ask any questions or show any interest. She listened quietly and went to her room to study. Suwei, who had usually felt hurt and dejected by her daughter's behavior, did not feel so anymore.

That night, Suwei opened her personal diary and noted the dates she met Miljana. She circled the three days March 25, April 1 and April 8. She smiled when she thought of the day they both danced together. She felt sad thinking of Miljana's mother and wondered what happened to her sister. Her mind was filled with questions, and she wanted to know all about Miljana.

Suwei spent the week looking forward to Miljana's visit, and waiting for the door bell to ring. She continued her usual chores and her routine lifestyle, without feeling sad or complaining to her brother. She eagerly waited for Miljana to come and take her shopping, as they had planned.

Chapter 7 - Day 4

It was Thursday, April 15th. Suwei had just finished her lunch and was tidying up the kitchen. She was listening to some Cantonese music and humming the songs when she heard the door bell. She ran to the door, expecting Miljana. She opened the door hastily and was overjoyed to see Miljana.

She was wearing the same blue skirt and a white t-shirt. She held out an assortment of beautiful orchids to Suwei and said, "Nënë, I got you some flowers." Suwei was touched by the wonderful gift. She thanked her and asked about her wounded knee. Miljana smiled and slightly lifted up her skirt to reveal the healing wound. Suwei was relieved to see that it had healed considerably.

She glanced behind Miljana onto the driveway, and not noticing the car, asked worriedly, "You could not get the car? Is your Uncle still upset?"

"No, that's O.K. We'll take the train" Miljana said dismissively. Suwei detected a sudden sadness in her voice. Not wanting to probe further, Suwei asked Miljana to wait while she got her things. Suwei went into the bedroom, changed quickly, grabbed her purse and the box of snacks she had set aside for them to take along.

Both walked to the station, laughing and talking about Melbourne's unpredictable weather and how people there could experience all four seasons in one day. They munched on the prawn crackers as they walked to the train station and boarded the train to Melbourne Central.

Suwei was exited to visit Melbourne with Miljana. She was happy in Miljana's company, who sounded upbeat and was once again radiating the charm that always captivated Suwei. Suwei knew that her own bereavement was nothing compared to Miljana's pain. Yet, she felt a strong connection of shared grieving.

They entered Melbourne Central and walked around, window shopping. They bought hot chocolate drinks at a café and enjoyed the music from the famous Cuckoo clock. Miljana was as excited as a toddler and squealed with glee to see the Cuckoo clock perform the chimes and the mechanized movements.

They shopped at Daimaru, where Suwei bought some clothes for Lin and Yen. Miljana bought a backpack for her school. Tired from all the walking, they decided to sit down for a while. They found a bench and settled down to quietly watch the crowded plaza. Miljana looked at Suwei and thanked her, "This is so nice. I always wanted to come here."

Suwei added, "I am enjoying the day too." She then asked Miljana in curiosity, "I wanted to ask you something. I always see you in the same dress. Why don't you wear another dress?"Miljana laughed heartily and with a sparkle in her eye, she said "This is my Thursday dress!"

Suwei realized that Miljana was a very beautiful young girl and was particularly charming when she smiled or laughed. She asked her what her name meant. "It means charming!" Miljana smiled.

"You are indeed charming! You should find a handsome young boy as a boyfriend, or do you already have one?" asked Suwei smiling at Miljana, who was blushing.

Evading the question, Miljana smiled and turned to look at the crowd in the mall. She turned back to Suwei and said softly, "Yesterday, I saw this boy at a store. He reminded me of my younger brother. Do you know my older brother joined the Kosovo Liberation army? He tried to kill my own father because he was a Serb!"

Suwei realized that Miljana wanted to talk about her past life again and wanted to share her thoughts. She was saddened to see Miljana slide again into the depression that seemed to be inextricably linked to her otherwise cheerful personality.

Suwei felt a pang of guilt as she realized that she was curious to learn more about Miljana, however painful it was for the young girl, to recount the horrible events that befell her family. Suwei's curiosity got the better of her and she asked, "What happened to your sister and mother? You cried a lot last week Miljana, and I felt very sorry for you. But I'm curious to know what happened. If it's OK with you, you can tell me."

As if on cue, Miljana said, "My sister Mirjeta went to get medicines for my mother. At that time, there was heavy bombing in Belgrade and Pristina; NATO was trying to control the war between the Serbs and Albanians. My mother was very sick and there were no doctors to see her. Mirjeta left my mother with Tatyana and went out bravely..." Miljana's thoughts trailed off, as she appeared to be staring at the people who were milling around the mall. She was far away in her strife-torn homeland reliving the horrors and tragedies she had witnessed there.

Miljana continued, "Mirjeta was very beautiful; she was taken away by some Serbian soldiers. My mother and sister waited for her several days and searched desperately for her. Nobody helped them. They tried to reach me, but we were hiding in bunkers." She paused again as her eyes welled with tears. Making a determined effort to continue and with a sudden burst of despair, she cried, "My sister was raped, again and again till she became pregnant. She was then sent to a refugee camp," Miljana bent her head, as though in guilt and shame.

She continued, "I was with my mother and younger sister Tatyana, when we were moved to a refugee camp. We found Mirjeta there. When we saw her, for the first time I felt we were really cursed. My mother died within days after she saw Mirjeta," said Miljana, tears flowing from her eyes.

Wiping her tears, Miljana looked at her watch and told Suwei she needed to return home to finish cooking for her Uncle and Aunt. Still in shock from what she just heard, Suwei held Miljana's hand and walked with her to the station to take the train to Clayton. Neither spoke a word. Suwei boarded the train to Clayton after tightly embracing Miljana and bidding her farewell. Promising to see her in a week's time, Miljana left.

Suwei sat in the train, still in a state of shock and her mind filled with questions. Miljana's past life affected her so profoundly that she started reflecting on her own feelings after her husband's demise. Suwei had continuously worried about Lin and her ability to cope with a single parent. Putting things in perspective, she now felt her daughter was very lucky and had a very good life. Her own confrontation with loneliness and boredom seemed trivial compared to the pain that Miljana endured after losing her family so miserably.

Suwei arrived home and prepared a quick dinner before Lin and Yen returned from school. That night after dinner, she went to Yen, who was reading in his bedroom. Not knowing how to explain about Miljana and unable to find the right words to start, she just sat there and cried. Thinking that his sister was remembering her husband and crying, Yen pacified her. Suwei was actually thinking of Miljana's life and the magnitude of sufferings that destiny had dealt this young girl.

Later that night, Suwei shuddered as she lay in bed thinking about Mirjeta and the plight of Miljana's mother. She prayed to Buddha for peace in the world and to grant security and happiness for women. She prayed fervently for Miljana's strength. Unlike any night before this, Suwei neither asked nor prayed for herself or her daughter.

Chapter 8 - Day 5

It was April 22nd, a week since Suwei had last met Miljana. She was anxiously awaiting a call or visit from Miljana. The anticipation made it difficult for her to eat. She kept imagining Miljana at the door in her usual blue skirt and white t-shirt and wondered what flowers she might bring her this time. She had no appetite for lunch, but started pouring out some soup, when she heard the bell ring. Elated, she ran to open the door.

It was Miljana in her usual Thursday dress, carrying a bouquet of long-stemmed blue iris and orange gerberas. "Welcome Dear, I was waiting for you!" Suwei gushed. Miljana handed the flowers to Suwei who admired the bouquet and thanked her. Both walked into the kitchen. Miljana asked Suwei, "Nënë, can you keep your food in the fridge? We can go out and eat. There is a wonderful Malaysian restaurant nearby. You have to eat their food, it's awesome!"

"Sure! I had not even started my soup! I will be ready in a minute," Suwei chimed in excitement and quickly dressed to go out.

It was a beautiful sunny day, and the temperature was just perfect for walking. Suwei talked about her daughter, "Lin was very caring and loving before we came here; she does not talk to me much now."

"I think she likes a Korean guy in school!" said Miljana with a sheepish smile and looked at Suwei who was shocked to hear Miljana's comment. Until recently, Suwei was so sure that Lin would have confided in her. She told Miljana how let down she felt about not knowing so many things that were happening with Lin and her school life. Miljana asked Suwei to let Lin take her own time to get accustomed to the change in life.

Soon they approached the small Malaysian restaurant and walked in. It was cool and pleasant inside, and they were seated at a table by the window. They ordered *Mee Goreng* and *Roti Canai*. They chatted continuously while enjoying the delicious food.

Miljana teased, "Lin is in love, so she will ignore you, Nënë! Seeing that she was still hurting from the news about her daughter, Miljana added, "She will want to share it with someone soon. When she realizes she is ignoring her mother, she will come back to you." Suwei nodded, trying to come to terms with the widening gap between them and hoping Miljana's words would come true soon.

"Did you know I had a boyfriend too?" Miljana remarked softly. Suwei looked at her, surprised. "I used to meet him in my English class in Belgrade! His father worked at the Chinese Embassy," she paused to see Suwei's reaction. Suwei asked "Was he from China?"

Miljana nodded, "Yes, from Beijing."

Suwei stopped eating and begged Miljana to tell more about her boyfriend. She was very excited to hear this and to see Miljana blush. "Chinese in Belgrade...? How did it happen?" Suwei asked eagerly.

"His name was Ma Chun, people called him Maachis. He was very smart. He travelled with his father who was a diplomat. He lived in London, Amsterdam and other places. I was so attracted to him; he was too," said Miljana with a smile as her cheeks turned red. He talked to me first. I remember he offered me *nian gao*. He said it was a Chinese New Year dessert.

"After that day, we met every Thursday for our English class. I taught him a lot of Albanian and Serbian words, he was a fast learner. One day he said *Ngo Oi Nai* to me," blushed Miljana.

"So he said he loved you?!" Suwei was still very excited.

"Yes, he did. He wanted to take me to a place where we could live peacefully. He always wanted to come to Australia; his sister lives in Melbourne." Miljana said. They were interrupted by the waiter who came by to serve their dessert, *Mango and Coconut Crème Caramel*.

As they enjoyed the Malaysian dessert, Suwei urged Miljana to continue. "He was the one who persuaded me to come to Australia, so he could follow me. One day we were returning home from school, when we heard gunshots. We quickly ducked into a nearby house. It was an abandoned house almost completely ruined by bombing," she said.

Staring at the dessert on her plate, Miljana said softly, "He kissed me. It was our first kiss and I really felt life was worth living. I forgot all my worries and for once, in a very long time, I felt safe and happy in his arms."

"The next week," she continued, "we went to Skadarlija. It is in an old bohemian quarter. We just wanted to be left alone, to hold each other and enjoy our time together. The few moments of happiness abruptly ended when we heard gunshots again and had to run for cover. Maachis was very scared for his life. He had several opportunities to leave Serbia, he did not. He wanted to stay with me," she stopped.

Suwei listened intently. She was now very curious to find out what happened after that, but was unsure how Miljana would react. They paid the bill and left the restaurant to walk back home. Miljana told Suwei that she had some work at school. Suwei hugged Miljana and expressed how happy she was to be with her. Suwei enjoyed her company immensely and did not feel the void of her daughter ignoring her. Suwei headed back home while Miljana went to the bus stop to catch a bus to school.

As Suwei walked, she imagined Miljana with a Chinese boy. She tried to picture a place filled with sounds of gunfire and people getting shot everywhere. She kept returning to the thought of how lucky she was. Her misery over the loss of her husband was nothing when compared to Miljana's life events. She felt bad for grieving all these days over what was lost, and not realizing the value of what she was left with.

When she returned home, Suwei made special food for her daughter and brother, people whom she loved and wanted to be happy. She was thankful that they were around and wanted to spend more time with them.

That evening, Suwei asked Lin to go for a walk. Though Lin was hesitant to accompany her mother, she relented after much persuasion. Suwei expressed her concern to Lin that she felt left out. Lin convinced her mother that she was engrossed in studying and apologized for being grumpy and distant. She wanted to do well in school and said that she found much comfort in her studies.

They both talked about Hong Kong, Tai Po and Lin's school. They remembered their friends and relatives in Tai Po and laughed recollecting some funny anecdotes from their past in Tai Po.

Chapter 9 - Day 6

Suwei was counting days and looked at the calendar every day, waiting for Thursday to arrive so she could see Miljana. On Wednesday April 28th, she was getting anxious and counting every hour. She could barely contain her curiosity. She wanted to ask Miljana about her Chinese lover, her mother and sister Mirjeta. That night Suwei could not sleep, her mind was once again filled with all the events Miljana had talked about the previous week.

It was finally Thursday, April 29th. Suwei was dressed in a light brown printed silk shirt and brown pants. She was hoping Miljana would come at noon as she usually did, so they could go out together. Miljana came just after noon. She was standing with a bouquet of long stemmed roses this time. She held out a box to Suwei and said smiling, "Good afternoon, Nënë. I got you some Belgium chocolates."

Miljana was dressed in the same blue skirt and white t-shirt. Her hair was let down and she was wearing a light red lipstick. Suwei gave Miljana a warm hug and said, "You are very charming; and also a very mysterious girl!"

Miljana suggested they visit the Carlton Gardens. Suwei agreed immediately. They took a train to Melbourne Central from Clayton and picked up *souvlakis* from a Greek take-away place. They got on the City Circle Tram to Carlton Gardens. This was the first time Suwei was riding in a tram. She had seen the trams as her brother drove them around the city, but had never taken a ride on one.

They visited the Royal Exhibition building and decided to take a stroll in the beautiful gardens. They walked through the dramatic tree-lined avenues and admired the Victorian-era landscape and street design, admiring the fountains along the way. Tired after all the walking, they stopped at a picnic area and sat down to eat their lunch.

Miljana noticed a couple of possums on a Eucalyptus tree and signaled Suwei to look at them. The possums were staring at their food. Miljana said, "These marsupials are so gifted, I envy them." Suwei noticed that Miljana was continuing to stare at the possums with her face turning red, as though she was reminded of something dreadful.

Suwei slowly put her hand on Miljana's shoulder and asked, "Are you OK, dear?" Miljana nodded her head and said, "My mother died in the refugee camp and Mirjeta died giving birth. Do you know Mirjeta means good life in Albanian? She never had a good life." Her eyes slowly moved towards the clear blue sky and she said, "As children, we always thought blessings came from heaven in the form of rain and snow but we never knew bombs would fall from the sky," she tried to smile as she continued to look at the sky. "We would flee to the shelters when we heard gunshots or saw anything fly in the sky!"

"Do you know Nënë, kids stopped flying kites there? Kids who once ran out to look at planes flying in the sky, ran away to hide at the mere sound of planes. Kids could tell a Mig-29 from a Nighthawk! My younger brother and his friends would look at the sky through the windows, waiting to get a glimpse of the stealth planes whizzing past, blissfully unaware of the fact that the planes dropped real bombs that killed real people. To them, it was like another Hollywood war movie. I can still remember the dead bodies and people crying everywhere after the bombing."

Suwei noticed that Miljana was continuing to look at the sky and urged her to eat and not think of the past. She tried to divert the topic, talking about Lin and how she had gone for a walk with her daughter and that they were now bonding very well. After a while, they decided to return home and walked through the Carlton Gardens in silence.

Suwei's mind was already occupied with questions, but she did not want to ask Miljana any more questions and make her feel worse. She could feel her pain and suffering and even though she knew more questions would bring out the painful memories, Suwei was once again tormented by this insatiable curiosity about Miljana's life. Throughout the tram ride to Melbourne Central, it was an effort for Suwei to restrain the torrent of questions that kept coming at her unabated. Silence only made it worse.

After their unusually quiet tram ride, Suwei bid Miljana farewell and took the train to Clayton. That night she was very depressed, her heart felt heavy and her mind was filled with dreary thoughts. She wore a warm sweater and jacket and sat in the front porch looking at the English Oak tree in the front yard. Lin was busy with her studies and Yen was watching the news on TV.

Suwei wondered why she had let her husband serve in the army. She pondered about her selfishness towards her immediate family needs, and indifference to the world around her. As she conjured scenes of bombed cities and human bodies from Miljana's descriptions, Suwei shuddered with guilt at the thought of her husband taking innocent lives when she could have stopped it. She detested having married someone who might have killed without remorse. Suwei found herself feeling a greater sense of relief than sorrow at the loss of her husband.

Suwei started spending every evening sitting at the front porch and staring at the English Oak. Though she appeared to be at peace in her surroundings, her mind was constantly occupied with conflicting thoughts. She wondered about Miljana's Chinese boyfriend, her father, brothers and sister. She smiled when she recollected Miljana's happy face and tears rolled out when the image of Miljana's sad face flashed in her mind.

Chapter 10 - Day 7

Suwei continued to grow eager and anxious as Thursday approached. She just couldn't wait to see Miljana. It was Thursday May 6th, and she felt her heart pound with joy and fear at the same time. She had not experienced this since the time of her delivery when Lin was born. They were the same contrasting emotions that had gripped her when as a kid, Lin was found after a frantic search at the beach. Lin had gone missing for a few minutes at the beach, but those were the longest and most tortuous moments of fear and trepidation Suwei had experienced.

Suwei now felt an incredibly powerful bond to Miljana - the same love she had for her mother and for Lin. She skipped breakfast and sat at the dining table as she stared at the clock waiting for it to turn twelve. As before, she wondered what flowers Miljana would bring this time.

It was barely a couple of minutes past twelve, and the door bell rang, Suwei ran to the door with joy. "Hello Nënë!" Miljana said chirpily, and gave her a bouquet of large oriental lilies. Thanking and hugging Miljana warmly, Suwei led her to the living room.

"I made some Chicken Chow Mein, let's have lunch. We can sit in the front yard in the shade." Suwei filled two Chinese bowls with Chow Mein noodles while Miljana transferred the lilies to a glass vase. They took two outdoor chairs and set a small table in the front yard under the English Oak.

As they enjoyed the lunch, Suwei took out a small box from her coat pocket and gave it to Miljana, who looked at it very surprised and opened it. There was a silver necklace inside with a small jade pendant of a laughing Buddha.

Not finding any words to say, she took the necklace out of the box and looked at Suwei with tears in her eyes and said, "I have not received any gifts like this for a long time." She immediately wore the necklace.

"You look so pretty, the laughing Buddha is to bring you happiness. I pray for your happiness," Suwei said admiringly.

Miljana smiled and talked as she looked at the pendant "Thank you Nënë. I want to be happy, I'm trying. You know, Maachis gave me a necklace one day. It was a beautiful one too. He came home that evening to talk to my father. He asked my father if he could take me to Australia. After a lot of persuasion and convincing, my father agreed."

Suwei listened intently and waited for Miljana to continue but Miljana paused for a long time and stared at the pendant. Unable to hold her curiosity Suwei blurted, "What happened dear! What happened to Maachis?"

"My father and Maachis drove with my younger brother to meet his father. NATO was bombing Belgrade and a bomb hit their car. Another bomb blasted the Chinese Embassy at the same time," she stared at the pendant as tears rolled out. She wiped her tears and continued to stare at the pendant in silence. Then with a sudden determination, she rose and said, "I have to go, Nënë. The food was great."

Once again, Suwei was in shock and blurted out, "Who is NATO? What happened to your other sister, Miljana?" Sue was holding Miljana's hand tightly, and was unable to contain her curiosity.

"I will come back tomorrow and tell you, Nënë. I have to go now. Thank you for this lovely gift." Trying to smile and putting on a brave face, she added, "Also, you will see me in a new dress tomorrow!" Miljana walked across the front lawn and crossed the street without turning back.

Suwei was transfixed after hearing Miljana tell about yet another tragedy that had befallen her. She was overcome with sorrow and sympathy for this young girl and wanted to comfort her. She rose from her chair and crossed the yard to the street. In despair, she watched Miljana walk very fast and disappear around the bend in the street. An unknown fear gripped her.

A couple of homes down the street, she heard children playing and shouting. Yet there was a haunting silence and she could hear the birds and the gentle afternoon breeze. Suwei feared if she had asked too many questions and kindled Miljana's misery. She sensed a dreadful foreboding and was almost convinced that something was wrong.

Suwei spent the entire evening in silence sitting on the front porch and staring at the English Oak. Lin was worried to see her mother's unusual behavior and tried to ask her why she was lost in thought. Yen asked her several times to come into the house as it was getting cold outside. Suwei simply shrugged off their concerns and remained outside, staring at the tree. After much persuasion, she went to her bedroom and lay on the bed, staring at the ceiling.

The next day was sunny and warm. But Suwei just stayed in bed. Thinking that she was unwell, Lin and Yen checked on her and pleaded with her to take rest. They reassured her that they would eat outside. Yen asked her not to sit outside in the cold till she feels better and left to school with Lin.

It was almost noon when Suwei got out of her bed and got dressed. She set a small table and two chairs in the front yard. She quickly prepared some soup and filled two bowls with soup and set it on the table. She sat there waiting for Miljana. Hours passed before Lin and Yen returned. They were disturbed to see Suwei sitting outside and staring at the English Oak with the untouched food in front of her. Worried about her mother, Lin persuaded her to go inside the house, but Suwei waved her hand dismissively, indicating to them to leave her alone.

At 7 pm, she walked into the living room and quietly sat next to her brother. Yen was worried about his sister and not getting any response to his repeated queries, he gave up the questions and offered her some fruit. Suwei started eating slowly as she stared blankly at the television.

It was the same news anchor. "Good Evening and welcome to Seven Nightly News. Today is Friday May 7th. We have breaking news from Belgrade. After forty-five days of continuous bombing by NATO forces in Serbia and Kosovo regions, the Chinese Embassy in Belgrade was bombed today. Initial reports indicate American bombs were used, raising tensions between the US and Chinese governments...."

Suwei stopped eating the fruit and her hands were trembling. She remembered Miljana mentioning that the Chinese embassy was bombed – she was confused, "This happened today. How could she...?" Suwei was gripped with fear and confusion. A chill went through her spine and she tried to speak, but there was no voice and she lost consciousness. Yen saw this and called out to Lin. He turned off the television and helped Suwei lie down on the couch. Lin rushed to her mother. They called the ambulance and took her to the hospital.

Chapter 11

It was June 10 1999, almost five weeks since Suwei last met Miljana. Suwei was sitting in the front yard and staring at the Oak tree. Lin and Yen made frequent trips to check on her.

Yen was watching television and the news anchor was reporting, "For the past few weeks, police in several towns in Victoria have reported a rather bizarre happening on Thursday afternoons. Middle-aged women have been sighted sitting motionless in their front yards or porches for several hours. According to reports coming in from several precincts, these women are mostly of Asian origin and are either housewives or widows. Some of the women who were questioned by police indicated they were waiting for a young girl to join them for lunch."

"Some of the families of these otherwise healthy women have approached doctors who have not found evidence or history of schizophrenia. In almost all the cases, these women seem to set lunch outside and wait for a girl to arrive on Thursday afternoons. The wait extends beyond late evening and this strange behavior has caused concern among neighbors. More on this after the headline update from Yugoslavia... today marks the end of NATO bombing operations in Serbia and Kosovo regions. Countless lives have been lost and several families displaced…."

Not wanting to listen to the war related news, Yen turned off the television and opened the front door. Suwei walked into the house and smiled at her brother and said, "I'm very hungry, let us eat!" Lin, who was in the kitchen cooking, came in to the living room and looked at her mother and smiled.